GUS DOESN'T ACT IN ANY OF the ways I expect a boy to act. He doesn't play rough. He doesn't pull my tail or try to pick me up.

Sometimes I watch him and I think maybe he's not looking at anything. Maybe the window is where he watches TV shows that only play in his mind. I don't know how I got this idea, but I watch his face and I think I might be right. His eyes change sometimes—like he's surprised one minute and laughing the next. Like a story is happening inside his head and the rest of us don't see it.

Also by Cammie McGovern

For Young Readers
Just My Luck

For Teens
Say What You Will
A Step Toward Falling

CHESTER
and
GUS

Cammie McGovern

HARPER
An Imprint of HarperCollinsPublishers

Library of Congress Control Number: 2016950346
ISBN 978-0-06-233069-7

Typography by Aurora Parlagreco
18 19 20   BRR   10 9 8 7 6 5 4 3 2
❖
First paperback edition, 2018

For our dearest Buddy

How to Tell Time

I'VE LIVED IN MY NEW HOME for three days but I still haven't met the boy I'm supposed to be best friends with.

He's nervous, I think.

So am I.

I don't know very many boys. I played with one once in the park where Penny brought me so I could get used to little children pulling on my fur and grabbing my tail. The boy in the park threw a ball and then a stick for me to fetch. When he got tired of that game, he said he was going to show me something called a slide that would be the most fun thing I'd ever done in my whole life. He picked me up and carried me to the top of it.

It was *not* fun. It was the opposite of fun. It was the most scared I've ever been except for the first time Penny practiced the "Dog Left Alone" test and tied me to a post for two minutes while she walked away. Afterward, she told me I wasn't supposed to whine or bark or show any signs of anxiety, which I didn't know at the time because I whined and barked like crazy. I couldn't help it. I was so anxious. This is what happens when you're a puppy. Your brain is so busy, you lose track of someone for a second and you think, *I haven't seen her for hours. She's probably dead.* You don't even know what dead is and you think it.

It's embarrassing now when I look back on it. I got nervous over lots of things back in those days.

When Penny came back, I dribbled pee I was so relieved to see her again! She knelt down and said, "It's okay, Chester. I was only gone two minutes," and I thought, *Really? Was it only two minutes? It felt more like two hours.*

I've never had a great sense of time and back then I wasn't completely sure what those words meant. Now I know. Two minutes is about the same as in a sec, and an hour means dinner's not for a long, long time, possibly days.

I loved our time at the park until that day the big boy carried me to the top of a slide and pushed me down. After that, I didn't love our trips to the park anymore.

Work

I KNOW I SHOULDN'T COMPLAIN ABOUT MY new home or this boy I haven't seen yet. It's my fault that I'm here, living with people who don't know their son very well if they got him a dog that he doesn't want to meet.

I was meant to be a service dog like my mother. She was a guide dog for a blind man until she got hit by a car, and then she retired to be a mother. "Being a mother is an important job, too," she told us, but she didn't really mean it. Having puppies made her tired and not very happy. Thinking about her old job made her happy.

"There's no better feeling than knowing there's one person in the world who depends entirely on you," she told us once. We were still small then and lying in a heap on top of each other. I had my brother Hershey's ear in my mouth. We all stopped what we were doing and listened.

"You meet your person and you *connect*. You learn what that person needs and you do it for them. It's the most satisfying feeling in the world."

After that we tried harder to pay attention during our puppy trainings. My sister Cocoa asked every person who gave us kibble or a drink of water, "Are you my person? Are *you*?"

Cocoa wasn't the smartest puppy in our litter. She was always eating things she wasn't supposed to.

One morning after breakfast, I looked up and saw a big group of people walking up the driveway of our farm. A few of them rolled in wheelchairs. One wore dark glasses.

Our people! I thought. *There they are!*

I ran to Cocoa and told her to come quick and look, but she was trying to eat a pinecone and didn't want to. My brother Hershey walked with me to the edge of our play yard and watched the group for a while.

Finally he said, "I want the big man in the rolling chair with pictures on his arms. You can have any of the others."

My heart started to beat faster. I didn't know how this worked—if we got to pick them or if they picked us. "Do we know enough yet to be paired with our person?" I asked.

"Yes," Hershey said. He was the biggest in our litter and

acted like he knew everything. "This is how it goes. Tomorrow we'll start our jobs. Remember, the man with pictures on his arms is mine."

For the rest of the morning, I worried. I thought about our mother's stories of her life with the blind man. *I did everything for Donald. I opened doors, I pressed elevator buttons, I guided him through traffic. Yes, I got hit by a car, but the important thing is: He didn't.*

There was so much I didn't understand. What was an elevator? What was traffic?

In the afternoon, we watched the people come outside with a group of dogs who were all wearing blue vests on their backs. Our mother came over to watch with us. When we pestered her with questions—*What are they wearing? What are they doing?*—she told us to be quiet.

"Just watch," she said. "This is the most important afternoon of their lives. They're being chosen by their person."

For the next hour, we watched them do tricks.

"Beautiful," our mother whispered under her breath. "Just beautiful."

"Sheesh," my brother Milton said softly. "That doesn't look like much fun."

"Fun isn't the point," Hershey snapped. "The point is getting someone to choose us."

I looked over at Hershey—his ears set forward, his nose working, taking it all in. I knew what he was thinking: *I want to wear a blue vest. I want to be chosen.*

I felt it too. We all did.

After the group went inside, we asked our mother more questions. "Learning all that will be the hardest thing you've ever done. You'll live with a trainer for almost a year and work constantly. That's all I can tell you. Even after all that work, some of you won't make it. That's just how it is."

She turned around and went back to her bed. That was that.

None of us knew what to think. Cocoa couldn't stop crying. "I don't want to *work hard*. I don't want to leave our play yard."

Milton was nervous, too. "What if we can't learn all those things?" By the end of the demonstration, the dogs were doing amazing things—finding and picking up tiny objects in the grass, holding a cane steady for someone who'd dropped it. "What if we can only learn about half those tricks?"

Hershey quieted him. "This is what we were born to do. It's our calling."

Cocoa whined some more.

"Don't be a crybaby," Hershey snapped.

In the middle of the night, I woke up and realized Cocoa was missing from our pile. I got the others up to help me look. We found her at the far end of our yard, lying on her side and moaning in pain, too sick to stand up. After Wendy, from the farmhouse, wrapped her up in a blanket and took her to the vet, our mother explained, "She ate three rocks last night. I have no idea why."

For a week we didn't see Cocoa, but we learned what the word "surgery" meant when Wendy told one of the workers: "Two hours of surgery. She had to have her stomach cut open and the rocks taken out."

When she finally came back, Cocoa seemed like a different dog—not really a puppy anymore.

A week later, she was given away.

"It's okay," our mother said, after she was gone. "Some dogs aren't cut out for the working life." She sounded as if we should all just forget about Cocoa for now.

I didn't of course. How could I?

Meeting Penny

HERSHEY WAS THE FIRST ONE TO be picked by a trainer and leave the farm. He didn't even look back as he got into the man's car. It was like he'd already forgotten his dog family, he was so ready to move on to the working part of his life.

After that, each of my brothers and sisters left one by one. I asked my mother if I should be worried that no trainer had picked me yet. "I don't know," she said. "Probably."

She wasn't a big one for reassuring her puppies. She didn't see the point. "Some of you won't make it as working dogs. That's all there is to it."

She didn't say Cocoa's name, but I thought of her of course.

After the last of my littermates was taken away and it

was just the two of us, my mother said, "They might think you're too much of a worrier." She snapped at a fly and went over for some water. "Try not to act so nervous the next time a trainer comes."

A few days later, I had my chance. Penny walked into our yard and right over to me. She wore a funny green hat and shoes with plastic flowers attached to them. "Look at you!" she said, reaching out to pick me up. "They must have saved the best for last!"

I wriggled and squealed and acted like a puppy again. I was so happy to be chosen I almost left without saying goodbye to my mother. At the last minute, I went over to the bed where she slept by herself now. "I have my trainer!" I said. "I'll see you in eight months! I'll work hard, you'll see! I'll try not to be too nervous, I promise!"

She confused me then, waking up from her nap, blinking at the light. "All right," she said. "I suppose it's too late now for anything else."

In the car, Penny told me all about herself. "Dogs are my true love, Chester. That's the first thing you should know about me. I've got no husband and no kids. Just a lot of wonderful dogs who I love and train and then I take them back to the farm to be matched with their person."

At her house, she showed me pictures of the dogs from her past in frames around her living room. Some of them looked like me in other colors, like yellow and black. "I've never had a chocolate lab like you. I think that's going to make you a little different from the rest."

She smiled as she said it and pulled me into her lap. I'd known her only a few hours and already she was nicer than my mother had ever been.

How to Be Understood

"EVERY DOG HAS A WEAKNESS," PENNY told me a few weeks into my training. "They're perfect in many ways and then suddenly, they see a rabbit in the woods and all their training goes out the window. Poof, off they go. If it's not a rabbit, it'll be something else. The trick is to figure out your challenge as early as possible, then work on it *a lot.* I've got a shelf full of windup squirrels if we need them."

I loved the way Penny talked to me all the time. I always answered, hoping she would understand me. *No thanks,* I tried to tell her that time. *I don't think squirrels will be my problem. I've seen lots of squirrels. I know not to chase them.*

I thought of what my mother had said and I wanted to be

honest with Penny. I looked her in the eyes. *I'm a little anxious sometimes. It might be a problem.*

She looked back at me and smiled reassuringly. "It's okay," she said, and for a second, I thought: *She understands! She knows what I'm saying!* Then she stood up. "I'm going to get one of those squirrels right now and try it on you."

A few days later, we discovered my weakness. After the boy carried me to the top of the slide. Penny worried that I might get scared of children, so she brought me to a school one morning and we sat outside the front door, saying hello to all the students as they walked in.

I was fine! Children were sweet! One girl lifted my ear and whispered, "You're the cutest dog in the whole world." Another girl lifted my other ear and said, "I love you!"

I love you too! I tried to say, but she didn't understand.

"No yipping, Chester," Penny said firmly, with a flat hand on my nose. It didn't hurt but still, I felt embarrassed. I had to remember that I understood what people said, but they couldn't understand me. I went back to the girls and licked their hands.

That's when it happened.

A terrible sound ripped through the air. My legs went jittery and frantic. I scrambled to get under a bench. *The sky is falling! The earth is blowing up!* I screamed to Penny, but she didn't hear me. How could she with all that noise?

When the noise finally stopped, I peeked out from the bench I was hiding under. I couldn't believe it. The children weren't scared at all! They even moved toward the door where the sound had come from.

After they were gone, Penny walked over to my hiding spot and crouched down. "That was just a school bell, silly dog. It looks like maybe loud sounds might be a problem, doesn't it?"

She talked softly to me the whole drive home. She told me it would be okay, that noises might hurt my ears but they couldn't hurt my body. She let me ride in the front seat next to her again, where she could keep a hand on my back. I was still having trouble catching my breath.

Her hand felt nice. So did her voice.

"We'll practice, that's all. When you don't expect it, I'll bang a few pots and pans and you'll get used to it. Caramel had this problem, too—you remember I told you about her? She got over it eventually."

That night while I ate my dinner, Penny dropped a cookie sheet on the floor. I thought it was a bolt of lightning hitting the house. I flew out of the room and under the sofa.

"Oh dear," Penny said from the kitchen. "Looks like we've got some work to do, Chester."

After that, we worked on it all the time. Along with heeling and fetching and opening doors, Penny and I practiced loud sounds. She whistled. She set off timers. Once, she deliberately set off her smoke alarm. She even warned me ahead of time as she held the match under the alarm. "This is going to be loud, sweetheart."

It was and I panicked. I knew I wasn't supposed to. Penny had told me many times: "When a loud sound comes, sit down and wait. Don't hide. Breathe in and out until it passes. Your person will need you. They have to be able to find you when it's over."

I knew all this and I still panicked. I couldn't help it. I ran as fast as I could and got under the closest bed or table I could find.

Except for this problem, my training went well. Almost every day, Penny told me how smart I was. One time, I knew what to do for a trick before she'd even taught me. The trick was opening a drawer and getting out a pot holder. It wasn't hard. I'd watched a dog do it on a DVD, but Penny must have forgotten, because after I brought it to her she said, "You might just be the smartest dog I've ever had."

After that, she did experiments to test my "vocabulary."

She put different objects around the room and asked me to fetch one without pointing at what she wanted.

"Please bring me my car keys, Chester," she'd say, and I could. That was easy because Penny misplaced them so much. Whenever she found them, she said, "I hate you, car keys! You always walk away!" I learned the word for "shoes" the same way and also "cell phone." Once she started those tests, I worked harder to remember the names of things because it made her so happy when I did.

It didn't seem like that much of an accomplishment to me until I heard Penny on the telephone with Wendy from the farm. "I've never seen such a young dog with such a big vocabulary. There are about fifty words that he's picked up entirely on his own. And it's not just that. He's six months old and he's already got so many commands down—heel, sit–stay, crate, go now, and don't touch."

Listening to Penny made me feel good.

"I've never seen a dog like this," she said. "He's remarkable, really. There's only one weak spot, I'd say. He seems to have a bit of sound sensitivity."

Those two words weren't in my vocabulary back then, but now they are.

Person Matching

THE FIRST TIME I SAW MILTON and Hershey again, they'd gotten so big I almost didn't recognize them. When I realized who they were, I was so happy, I ran right over. "We're getting matched with our people! It's finally going to happen!" I think they were excited too, but were trying not to show it. We were back on the farm and we'd just visited our mother, who gave us a sniff and turned around. Maybe that was her way of saying, *You're older now. Don't act like puppies.*

I felt excited and nervous and also a little sad. On the drive that morning, Penny had said, "Chess, I have to tell you that if someone picks you this weekend, you'll stay here for the next two weeks and train with them. You won't come home with me."

I knew this would happen sooner or later and it would be the saddest part about becoming a real service dog. I loved Penny more than I'd ever loved anyone. I couldn't imagine leaving her, but recently I'd come up with a new idea where maybe I wouldn't have to. My plan was to get matched with someone Penny could fall in love with. Then she could marry that person and we could all live together afterward!

It was a great idea except it made me extra nervous meeting the group. I tried to avoid going near the people who looked like they were already married, but that was hard to figure out. I definitely avoided the three children in the group. I knew Penny felt uncomfortable with children, so I didn't think she'd want to marry one.

At demonstration time, each dog and trainer pair were given five minutes. Hershey and Milton used more time than they should have showing off tricks. When it was my turn, there wasn't much time left.

Penny and I walked out to the middle of the group. Across the yard, I saw my mother and I thought about Cocoa, who'd wanted her own person, too, but couldn't stop eating things she wasn't supposed to. I heard my mother's voice: *Some dogs aren't meant to do this work. That's just how it is.*

I looked at the strangers sitting in the chairs. "Okay, Chester, are you ready?" Penny whispered.

17

Panic rose up from my stomach to my throat. *No,* I told her. *I don't want to leave you.*

"Heel," she said.

I did.

"Sit."

I did.

"Stay, please."

I did.

"That's a good dog," Penny said, crouching down to hug me. Then she stood back up to talk about me to the group like the other trainers had about their dogs. "Chester is a highly intelligent, very sensitive dog. I've trained seven dogs now, and there are many ways in which he's different from any of the others."

I could tell she was nervous. She kept wiping her hands on the front of her skirt.

"From the very beginning, I noticed that Chester seemed to understand certain words before I'd ever taught them to him. I've done some research about canine language acquisition and discovered that some unusual dogs can pick up on our speech even when they aren't being directly addressed or trained. When tested, some of them have a vocabulary of up to five hundred words or more."

I saw Wendy in the back of the circle point to her watch.

Penny kept going: "Anyone who chooses Chester should know that he currently has a working vocabulary of at least three hundred words along with the ability to *infer* meaning, which I've never seen in a dog before. If I lay out three objects, two of which are known to him, and ask him to select one with a name he doesn't recognize, he'll infer that it must be the item he doesn't know. This is almost unheard of in the animal kingdom outside of chimpanzees and gorillas. I've talked to some canine behavior scientists who've told me they'd like to meet Chester."

I was proud to hear all this, but also worried. She'd gone on for so long, it was a little embarrassing. Milton snorted in boredom. Hershey yawned.

Also, she was *telling* people how smart I was rather than having me show them.

Finally Wendy thanked Penny and told her our time was up. "Our guests need a chance to meet these dogs and get to know them one on one. Trainers, if you don't mind, we'll ask you to move around the room and give each person here a chance to interact with your dog—"

"I just have to say one more thing," Penny interrupted. "Chester is an extraordinarily smart dog, but he is also a little sound sensitive. He overreacts to loud, unexpected sounds. We've worked on it a lot, but I'm not sure how much better it's gotten. There. I just had to say that."

Wendy smiled at Penny, but it wasn't a real smile. "Fine then. Thank you, Penny."

"It's not *that* intrusive. He's fine with telephones and microwaves. He has a hard time with sirens and thunderstorms."

"Yes, okay. Thank you again, Penny."

After that, we moved around the room like the other dog/trainer pairs, but no one reached out to pet me or ask any questions. One man whose wife was in a wheelchair asked Penny what sort of words I knew. "Well, nouns, mostly," Penny said. "I test him by laying three objects on the floor and asking him to fetch one."

"And you don't think he looks at your eyes to figure out which one you're after?"

"No," she said, but I could tell she was surprised, like maybe she hadn't thought of this before. "I don't think so."

"Dogs are pretty good at reading people's *faces*. Understanding what we're *saying*, I'm not so sure about."

"Oh, Chester understands. I know he does. I could do a demonstration right now. If I lay out a towel, a sock, and a shirt and ask for one, he'll get it right eighty-two percent of the time."

She was talking too fast and her face was red. She wanted people to like me, but instead they were moving away from her. I didn't blame them exactly. These people were in wheelchairs mostly. They needed different kinds of help. They weren't interested in my vocabulary.

I watched Hershey, who'd obviously found the person he'd always dreamed of: a burly, tattooed man in a wheelchair. They already loved each other, I could tell. Milton had also found his person—a gray-haired woman who used a walker. He sat beside her, with his chin raised for a scratch. She was bent over, talking softly to him.

It had been less than an hour, but already each person had picked out their dog. The only leftovers were me and Grendel, a high-strung poodle waiting to be matched with a dog-allergic person.

I worried that Penny might start to cry in front of the group. I smelled tears coming. I nudged her with my nose and then my whole face. *It'll be okay,* I said. *I get to go home and stay with you now! We'll come back and try again next month!*

She didn't hear me of course.

Now I understand that something more was going on.

Penny wasn't about to cry. She was mad. She was also watching the sky, and the dark clouds rolling in. She knew what was coming before anyone else out in the yard did. She saw the jagged finger of lightning. I don't know why she didn't move to get us inside before the explosion, unless maybe she knew what would happen and wanted it to transpire exactly as it did.

These people had already chosen the dogs they wanted and I wasn't one of them.

They'd already rejected me.

Maybe she thought: *We'll stand right here and make sure we never have to go through this again.*

The next thing I knew, thunder cracked above us. I thought the sky had exploded. I thought the world was ending. I scrambled to the nearest cover I could find, a ramp outside my old play yard. I shut my eyes for a long time.

When the noise finally stopped, I opened my eyes. Three puppies and my mother were staring at me.

"What's wrong with him?" they asked my mother.

"Never mind him," she said, walking away.

When Penny finally found me, she said only, "Come on, Chester, we're *going.*"

We walked to her car past a half dozen dogs getting to

know their new person on the porch. It was raining by then but we were the ones getting wet. My brothers didn't look at me or say goodbye. Wendy called out to Penny, "We'll be in touch!"

Penny kept walking.

"Never mind these people," Penny said when we got into the car. "I mean it, Chester. You're too smart to do this work. You're too good for all of them. We're going home."

How to Communicate

PENNY STAYED AWAKE LATE THAT NIGHT reading about Chantek, an orangutan who learned sign language, and Rocky, a sea lion who did math problems with his flippers.

"I never knew how smart animals could be, Chester. It's amazing. Bring me my red reading glasses, would you?"

She'd forgotten that colors were hard for me. I brought her one pair. "Not those," she said. "The red ones." She was hunched over the computer, squinting at typeface.

I found another pair and hoped for the best.

"There they are! Thank you!"

The more she read, the better she felt about what happened at the farm.

"This could turn out to be the best thing that happened

to either one of us. If you'd found a match there, you would have spent the rest of your life working for someone else. Instead we can focus on you, and getting the world to recognize how smart you are."

She kept reading for most of the afternoon. By the end of the day she had a plan worked out. "I've just found out there are dogs who can be taught to read. At first you do it by reading commands off prompt cards. Once you get the idea, we keep building in new words until you have the reading vocabulary of a first grader! Then I put up a wall of words and when there's something you want to tell me, I'll attach a laser pointer to your head that will read the words as you look at them. Think about it, Chess—you'll be able to talk!"

I wasn't sure about this. How would reading help me be a better service dog? Were there people with disabilities who used flash cards, not words? I hadn't seen anything like that in the videos we watched, but maybe there were.

For the rest of the day, we worked on the first card she wanted me to learn. It had "SIT" written in large black letters.

"Siiiiiit," she said, holding up the card. She pointed to the word and drew it out.

I sat, of course. My rump knows only how to follow

orders. Next, Penny pulled out the same sign again and said nothing.

I sat again. It wasn't hard to make Penny happy. She squealed and clapped and showered me with kisses.

Over the course of the afternoon, she made up three more signs, each one written in a different color ink on a different color paper. Even if I had trouble with my colors, it wasn't hard to memorize what each card looked like. "STAY" was in big black letters. "SHAKE PAW" was in smaller letters. "BANG" was on a card with a folded corner.

I wasn't really reading them of course. Dogs can't read words. But we know how to please people. When Penny explained what "BANG" meant and showed me the trick, that was easy too. By the end of the day, I'd mastered all four cards. Penny was thrilled.

"You're already better than Willow! She can read only three commands and she made it onto *Good Morning America*!"

All this excitement made Penny a little breathless when she answered the phone that evening. "Yes, hello, Wendy! We're fine," I heard her say. "Better than fine, in fact! I've just taught Chester to read four words."

I hoped Penny wouldn't go on or say the part about how I might learn to talk soon using a laser pointer attached to my head. I knew Wendy would think it sounded silly. Penny didn't say anything about that—instead, she went quiet for a while.

"But I don't understand. I assumed Chester would have another chance to find a match . . . Are you saying that because no one picked him that one time, he has no chance of being a service dog—"

Wendy must have cut her off. The next thing I heard was: "I won't do that, Wendy. It's not right. I told you I'm happy to keep him for now."

I didn't understand what was happening until she hung up and called her sister. By then, she was crying. "She's telling me I can't keep Chester—that I should read my contract, which says if he fails the qualifying test or can't find a match, they'll place him with a suitable family. Legally he's theirs! I'm not allowed to keep training him!"

I wasn't sure why this surprised her when she'd been telling me all along that this would happen. "You won't live with me forever, Chester. I wish you could but that's not the deal."

"They obviously don't care about him. Apparently a family will pay eight hundred dollars for a service dog reject. All they care about is the money!"

She turned away from me as she yelled into the phone.

I never understood that. Penny had spent so much time

confirming how much language I understood—then she said things like that right in front of me.

That night, Penny invited me onto the sofa and showed me the video clip of Willow's appearance on *Good Morning America*. "Maybe this will cheer us up. This dog is famous like you should be."

After I watched it, I understood. Dogs don't learn to read to help people. They learn to read to get on TV. Penny wanted to show up Wendy and the others on the farm who had made her so nervous at our demonstration.

Realizing all this didn't make me love Penny less—it only made me wish I could read her words and talk to her using a word wall and a laser. Then I could tell her that she didn't need to try so hard or get so nervous. We didn't *need* to be on TV for people to like her. I loved her and I knew other people would too. *If we could just relax and be ourselves, every-thing will be okay.*

That's what I would have said to Penny if I could talk in words she understood.

But I couldn't of course, so I just sat beside her and watched videos of people pretending their dogs could read.

Mysterious Boy

A FEW DAYS LATER, SARA AND MARC came to visit.

"We have a little boy, Gus, who can't wait to meet you," Sara said, getting down on the floor beside me.

Marc laughed, sounding a little nervous. "I don't know about that. We have a boy who's not sure how he feels about dogs, so we're hoping to get a really nice one."

Penny was in the corner of the kitchen, not saying anything.

"He needs a friend like you," Sara whispered. "We love him so much, but it's not easy figuring out how to be his friend. He doesn't really like other people very much, especially other kids, so we're hoping, maybe with the right dog—"

I liked these people fine, but they didn't seem like the right match for me. Especially the part about having a boy at home. I thought about the boy who carried me up the slide. Boys made me nervous.

"He's not great with children," Penny said.

I was surprised. It was the first mean thing I'd ever heard her say about me.

Sara seemed surprised too. "Really? He seems like he's got such a gentle disposition. Like he'd be *great* with kids."

"Maybe I should say he hasn't spent a lot of time with them. I tried, but both times we had incidents that left him pretty scared. It's hard for me to say how he'd react around a group of children."

I thought about my one time sitting in front of the school, with all the girls hugging me and whispering in my ear before the bell rang. I liked that part. I really did.

"I don't know," Sara said. "Maybe this is crazy, but I have an instinct this is the right dog for us. Don't you feel it too, Marc? Look at his eyes. Don't you think Gus will fall in love?"

"I don't know, sweetheart. *Maybe.*"

"I think I'll call Wendy and tell her we've found him. This is the one we want."

I could tell Penny was upset. She didn't want me to go with these people. "Maybe I should come out to your house and meet your son. Just to get a better sense of the situation."

"Okay," Sara said and looked at Marc. "Is that how it's done?"

"I could help Chester get settled and show you what he can do. I know he's not an official service dog, but he's so capable, he ought to be able to use all his skills."

"Oh, we'd love that Penny! What a nice offer! That sounds great."

That night, Penny and I sat together on the sofa for our last dinner and evening of watching TV together. I knew she was sad. So was I.

"I don't know if these are the right people for you, Chester. That's why I asked to come out to their house. I can't bear to think of you ending up with a family who wastes your gifts. I promise that if I get a bad feeling while we're at their house, I'm going to do whatever I have to to get you back."

I knew how sad she was. I put my head in her lap and licked her hand. I thought about my mother, who didn't care when I left. *I promise I'll make you proud!* I tried to tell

31

Penny. *I'll use everything you taught me. People will see me and know I had the best trainer in the world!*

The next day Penny drove me over to their house. I wanted us both to be brave. I didn't want them to think Penny was strange or nervous the way Wendy did.

"I'm going to tell them you can read," she announced in the car. "I want them to know that it's a possibility for you. Maybe I'll show them the videos of Willow."

I'm not sure that's a good idea, I tried to tell her with my eyes.

"Obviously they won't have as much time to work with you on it as I did, but I still think they should know."

When we walked into the house, the first thing Penny said was "I've brought some flash cards I've been using to teach Chester how to read. I know that might sound crazy, but there are professionals out there who say teaching dogs to read is the best chance we have to achieve real communication between dogs and people. I think Chester is capable of this. I've never known a dog who is so intelligent."

Sara and Marc looked at each other. "Okay," Sara finally said.

Penny kept going: "I understand that you're adopting him into your family, but I'd like him to have a chance to realize his full potential. That's all."

"Why don't you give us the flash cards and whatever other material you have? It sounds great. I'm happy to look through it."

Penny looked confused. She thought about it for a minute and then said, "Do you mean it or are you just saying that?"

"Oh, I mean it! A dog who can read! How exciting. We had no idea."

Penny smiled. I could tell she liked Sara more now and didn't care when Sara went upstairs and came back down to say, "I'm so sorry about this, but Gus is feeling too shy to come out of his room right now."

She didn't wonder what that meant or worry that it might be a bad sign. Instead she sat down with Sara and told her more about my reading program. I didn't listen to that part. I was wondering why a boy wouldn't come down and meet his new dog. The more I thought about it, the stranger it seemed. Why hadn't he come with his parents to Penny's house? Then I got an idea: Maybe he was in a wheelchair! If he was and I ran into Milton, he would think I was a real service dog and not just a family pet! In fact, he didn't have to be in a wheelchair. Maybe he could be blind or deaf. Just someone with problems that I could help with. That's what I hoped.

After a while, it was time for Penny to go. She hugged me and said she would never forget me. I told her what I'd been thinking: *If this boy has problems, maybe I can help him!*

Penny turned to Sara. "It looks like maybe he has to go to the bathroom. This is his look for 'Can I please go outside?'"

It was sad, really, how little Penny understood me. I loved her so much, but I don't think that's enough for people to understand what you're trying to say.

Freezing Like Statues

THIS MORNING I MET MY BOY.

His name is Gus and he came into the kitchen before anyone else was awake. His pajama pants smelled like urine,
which I loved. All dogs love this smell. To us, it smells
like a friendly hello. I went closer to smell it better and he
screamed so loud I ran back to my bed in the corner.

A second later, Sara came into the kitchen and turned on
the light. "Gus, baby, it's okay," she said. She almost hugged
him, then came over to my bed and hugged me instead.
"It's okay, Gus. This is Chester. You remember we told you
about Chester coming to live with us."

He stopped screaming and started making a high-pitched
squealing sound that hurt my ears and must have hurt his

too, because his hands were covering both of them.

I wished my paws could cover my ears.

Sara kept talking to him. "Shh, baby. Calm your body down. Breathe in and out. Chester isn't going to hurt you."

She kept talking like that. Calmly. Saying "Shh . . ." in between her words.

Eventually Gus started to listen. His hands came down from his ears.

"That's good, baby. You're calming yourself down." Sara held her breath and then kept going. "Good for you, brave boy. Do you see that you're okay? You're in the same room with Chester and everything's okay?"

I could tell this made her happy.

When Marc came in, he and Sara made silent, happy faces at each other.

Marc held out one hand, close to Gus's shoulder, but didn't touch him. "I'm proud of you, Gus. You're very brave," he said.

I didn't move at all.

Judging by the way Sara and Marc held still, I thought: *Maybe it's not me he's scared of, it's anything that moves.* We stayed like that for a long time. Frozen like statues. Marc's hand reaching out, almost touching Gus's shoulder but not quite.

None of us looked at each other. None of us were sure what to do next. Eventually we moved again, because of course we had to breathe and eat breakfast and all of that.

Windows and Movies

I'VE SEEN GUS TWICE NOW AND, though he walks a little funny, he doesn't use a wheelchair. He's also not blind and he isn't deaf. Still, I can tell he's different from other boys. For one thing, he doesn't talk. He *can* talk, I think, he just never does, except a little bit to himself. I don't think he means for anyone else to hear him, because once he said three words together and Sara stopped what she was doing and clapped. "Nice talking, Gus! That was from the movie we watched last week! What made you think of that, I wonder?"

Gus got up and left the room. I think it was an accident that she'd heard what he was thinking.

I watched this from my bed in the kitchen and thought:

He has the opposite problem as me. I have thoughts I want to say and can't. He has thoughts he wants to keep inside and can't.

Mostly, though, he never talks.

Instead of talking, he screeches or chirps or just moans softly for a long time. Sara calls it droning. "No droning in the living room, babe," she'll say. "Mom is trying to work and it drives Mom crazy while she's trying to work, remember?"

Usually he doesn't stop.

"Gus?" she'll say. "Do you hear me? No droning down here. If you have to drone, go up to your room."

He still doesn't stop.

"GUS! I'M GOING TO COUNT TO THREE . . ."

Then it's like his brain *is* listening, because if she says she's counting to three, he stops. He doesn't want her to count to three. I keep my head down but I watch all of this carefully.

Except for Gus's droning sounds, it's quieter here than it was at Penny's. No one watches TV all the time the way Penny did. Gus spends most of his day standing at a window in the living room, staring out at the front lawn and a tree. I sit behind him to see what he's looking at, which isn't much. I'm not sure why he looks out the window when nothing changes or seems to happen out there. It's late summer, so there's no wind and even the leaves don't move really.

At Penny's house, the TV was on almost all the time, which I loved. TV shows helped me learn a lot about people. Penny was a big fan of detective shows and mysteries, and she would explain what was happening as they went along. "A lot of times, the criminal is a person who seems really nice at first. Sometimes even old ladies are killers. It's who you don't *expect*," she once told me.

I didn't know what "expect" meant when she first said it. Now I do. I can even use it in a sentence: Gus doesn't act in any of the ways I expect a boy to act. He doesn't play rough. He doesn't pull my tail or try to pick me up.

Sometimes I watch him and I think maybe he's not looking at anything. Maybe the window is where he watches TV shows that only play in his mind. I don't know how I got this idea, but I watch his face and I think I might be right. His eyes change sometimes—like he's surprised one minute and laughing the next. Like a story is happening inside his head and the rest of us don't see it.

How to Not Scare Someone

GUS STILL DOESN'T LIKE BEING IN the same room with me, but these days he doesn't scream if he walks into a room and I'm here. Instead he turns his face away from the corner where I'm lying. I try to make myself small. I don't move, because moving scares him most of all. Moving makes him remember that I'm here and I'm unpredictable, and I'm pretty sure he wishes both those things weren't true.

I haven't been here very long, but I'm starting to think maybe I *do* have a job after all. If Gus is scared of me because I move, that means he must be scared of a lot of things that move, like cars and bicycles and balls and people. I think helping Gus not be afraid of me could be my job.

I try an experiment. After dinner, instead of staying as far away from Gus as possible, I go upstairs quietly while Sara helps him get ready for bed. I don't go into his room. I stay in the hallway outside his door and watch as Sara holds puffy underwear open for him to step into, then his pajama bottoms. After he gets into bed, he sits up on his pillow and rocks so hard his head hits the wall.

It's hard to watch. It looks like it hurts, but Sara doesn't stop him. She lets him do it for a while and then she puts her hand on his shoulder. "Shh, baby, shh . . . ," she says. "Roll over on your tummy, sweetheart. I'll rub your back."

He stops banging and rolls over, like this is something they do every night.

Sara sits down on the edge of his bed. She hums softly and pats his back in the same rhythm that he was banging his head. As his body calms down, I realize it's the rhythm, not the banging that he likes. I try moving my tail to the same beat.

Maybe this will help, I think. If I practice, I can help him get to sleep like Sara does.

Then Gus's eyes open at the sound of my tail. This is a mistake. He sees me at the door and I feel terrible. Sara is tired. She wants to go to sleep too but she can't until Gus falls asleep. And now he's awake again, staring at me.

I get ready for a scream.

If he screams, I'll scramble myself back downstairs as fast as I possibly can. I'll say sorry a million times in my head to Sara. I'll promise never to come near Gus's room again.

I'm so nervous I look away. Another rule with Gus is he doesn't like looking people in the eye. If you do, he always looks away like it hurts his eyes. But this time, I'm surprised: When I peek up for a second, his eyes are still open and they're looking at me.

He's seeing me and he's not screaming.

He doesn't mind that I'm sitting in the hall outside his door.

He's not smiling but he's not minding either.

He's looking at me and I'm looking at him and it's okay. He doesn't mind my being here. Which makes me feel like maybe I've just done a pretty good job.

A New Idea

❖

———————————————

GUS IS DEFINITELY GETTING USED TO me. Sara notices it too.

In the morning as Marc gets dressed for work, she asks if he's noticed. I don't know what Marc does for a job, but he smells like wood and sawdust and sometimes paint. I love how Marc smells. I love that he hardly ever washes his pants. He takes them off next to the bed and in the morning he steps back into them. When he says, "I guess so. Maybe," Sara says, "It's making me think about that idea I had. I called the school yesterday and asked if they'd be willing to consider having Chester in school with Gus a few hours a day, and they're willing to at least talk to me about it! Mr. McGregor told me to stop by."

I can tell Marc is surprised by the way he looks up. "The principal?"

"Yes! We'd have to get it approved by the new teacher and also have to make sure no child in his classroom has an allergy . . ."

"Did you tell him that Chester's not an official service dog?"

"I did some research and it turns out those rules are a lot looser than I thought. There are all kinds of service dogs and there's no official licensing test or anything like that. You just have to prove that the dog performs a necessary task that the disabled person can't perform for themselves. SDI is a private organization that only certifies its best dogs but the state doesn't mandate any certification. I read a whole forum online last night. A lot of people said they'd used their SDI dropout dogs as regular service dogs. Some of them turned their old dog-in-training vests inside out and no one ever asked a single question."

Marc shakes his head. "I don't know, Sare—"

"Chester *wants* to work, Marc. I watch him all day and I can tell. He'll bring me things he thinks I've lost, like socks and car keys. It's like he spends all day showing me everything he can do. During the day when you're gone, every time I turn around he's sitting behind me, waiting for an assignment. Sometimes I ask him to get my keys just so he feels useful."

Now I feel embarrassed, of course. I'd wondered about all the key-fetching I'd done. I thought maybe her office was full of locks.

"I'm not saying he'd have to go to school every day. Maybe he'd go a few mornings a week. I just want to *try* something that will make this year better than last year."

"I don't want to start making a lot of demands on the school again if we're not sure it'll do any good. Last year they spent a lot of money on a talking computer that Gus refused to learn how to use."

"But we had to *try* it, right? He's a nonverbal ten-year-old. We have to try every alternative communication form while he's still young enough to learn it."

"Look, Sara, what would we be trying to accomplish by sending Chester into school with Gus? He still makes Gus nervous. I'll admit he's gotten better but it's not like they have some magical bond."

"You're not home all day with them—you don't see what I do."

"What do you see? Does Gus ever go over to him? Or

voluntarily interact with him?"

"Not exactly, but there's something happening below the surface. I *feel* it. Gus is aware of Chester and it's making him more aware of other things, too."

"Like what?"

"I'm not sure how to describe it."

"Is he using any new words?"

"No. He repeats a little more but he doesn't use any new words."

"Does he respond when you ask him to do something?"

"Not really. Not without counting to three."

"So what's different?"

"Well—maybe this will seem silly, but sometimes I'll see Gus at his window and Chester sitting behind him. Then I'll look again, maybe half an hour later, and they're both still in the exact same position, only Gus has turned his body a little bit so Chester can look out the window too. Like he's *aware* of Chester and he doesn't want to block his view."

It's funny that she noticed that. I noticed it too. That's how I figured out Gus isn't really looking out the window, because there's nothing there. He's doing something else but I don't know what it is.

"And you think that's significant? That he moved two inches for the dog?"

"I think it's significant that they stayed in the same room together for a half hour without moving more than two inches. Yes, I do."

Marc sits down on the bed beside her. "I think Chester is a very sweet dog who's been trained to sit for two hours without moving if his person needs that. I'm not sure it means anything except he knows how to sit still for a long time."

"But think about it, Marc. He's never been told that he's supposed to work with Gus. He figured it out himself. Doesn't that tell you that he *wants* this job? I don't know if this is the answer, but I feel like we have to try *something*." There's so much emotion in her voice, I go closer and put my head in her lap, the way I always did with Penny.

Marc scoots closer to her. He can't stand to see her cry either, but he can do more than I can, because he has arms. It's nice to see him hug her. It makes me wish I had arms too.

How to Build a Nest

THE MINUTE I HEARD SARA'S IDEA yesterday, I started to get nervous. All morning while Sara's at school talking to the principal, I think about my problems. Being too anxious. Overreacting to loud sounds. These are bad problems to have, but they also mean I understand what Gus feels like. I know why he puts his fingers in his ears when things get loud and noisy. I only wish I could do the same thing with my paws.

I also know what it feels like when your body does things you don't want it to, like run under a bed during a thunderstorm. Gus doesn't do this, but I do. I can't help it. I just have to get under something. During a thunderstorm, Gus does other things like rock back and forth on his toes and flap his hands and hold his sparkly pen up to the corner of his eye. That's his way of hiding under the bed. He gets very loud and tries to do all his favorite things at once so his body will calm down.

Gus is scared of a lot of things. I smell it all the time. Whenever he hears an unexpected sound. Whenever I bark or even just walk past his room with my toenails clicking the floor. Noises hurt his ears and I make too many of them. I wish there was a way to promise him I won't ever bark at school, but there isn't. He'll be anxious all the time, his fingers ready to jam into his ears, in case I bark.

I want this job, but I'm afraid Marc might be right. This isn't the right job for a dog to have. I don't think Gus needs a dog, he needs a world that is very quiet and a family who will let him do exactly what he wants to do all day long, which is look out the window.

I don't know what he thinks about when he stares out the window, but that's when he smells the happiest. It's the only time, really, when he smells calm. The rest of the time, he smells nervous. Doing everything Sara makes him do—going on errands, helping her cook dinner, taking me for a walk—he doesn't like any of it. It all makes him anxious.

He loves his mom, but he knows he can never make her happy, which is sad for him, I think. I'm not sure, because

I can't smell quiet emotions underneath the surface. I can only smell big ones.

I remember when we were getting ready to return to the farm to test my skills and maybe find a match for me, Penny said she was sure I would pass the tests, she had no doubts at all. "The main question will be pairing you with the right person. You can be the best dog in the room, but you still need to find the right match. That's what I'm most nervous about."

Now we know she should have been nervous about a few other things, too. Now I know wanting a job isn't the same thing as being able to do it.

Sara is at the school for a long time, talking to them about letting me come to class while Marc stays home with Gus and me. Sitting behind Gus, staring out his window, I've noticed something interesting: A pair of birds is building a nest on the front porch. I don't understand what they're saying because bird noises are hard for a dog to interpret. It seems like they're fighting most of the time, but still, by the end of the morning, they've got a nest in the rafters for the mother to lay her eggs in. I can only imagine how accomplished they must feel. They had a job and they did it.

It gets me wanting to feel the same way.

Something to Love

"THEY SAID YES!" SARA SCREAMS THE minute she walks in the door. She's very happy—clapping her hands and laughing. "Everyone was so nice! It's like they still feel bad about last year or something."

What happened last year? I want to ask. I walk over to Sara and put my head in her lap so maybe she'll say what happened last year.

She doesn't.

"Did you tell them he's not an official service dog?"

"I called him a therapy dog, which is different. He'll just spend a few hours a day at school, helping Gus socialize with other kids."

"And they were okay with that?"

"Yes!" Sara smiles. "I told them if there were any problems I'll come right back and pick him up. We're going to be very flexible about it all."

Marc makes a face like he's not too sure.

"Oh, Marc. Don't imagine problems before we've had any."

"Okay—so did you meet the new teacher?"

"Her name is Marianne Winger and she seems great. She didn't spend our whole first meeting talking about how to manage behaviors, which I loved. She asked a lot of questions about what Gus loves and what his passions are."

"What did you tell her?"

"That was the problem. I almost said Thomas the Tank Engine, but he hasn't played with those for years, has he? Her question got me thinking: We don't really know what he cares about anymore, except staring out the window."

Marc thinks about this. "He's calmer these days, which must mean he's happier, right? It's hard for us to guess what's going on in his head."

"No, I know. I just wish he'd find something that he loves, that's all. The way he used to love trains."

I think about all the things I love: chew toys, mostly. Balls. Food. Penny, who I love and still miss. I know Gus well enough now to know balls aren't his passion. Though I've seen him chew the collar of his shirt, I don't think chew toys would be a good bet. This gives me something to work on at school, though. Maybe I can help him find something he loves.

Expectations

I'VE NOW HEARD THE WORDS "FIFTH grade" so many times, I thought maybe it was the name of Gus's school.

"You're going to have fun in fifth grade!" Sara says.

"Chester is going to love fifth grade and so are you, Gus!"

"In fifth grade, the subjects get really interesting! You'll finally get to study American history! Remember how you loved our trip to Williamsburg? And the Freedom Trail in Boston with the man dressed up like Paul Revere?"

Sara says all this as Gus eats his breakfast on the first day of school. I try to tell her with a nudge of my nose into her knee, *Too much talking for the morning. Better to be quiet and let Gus get himself ready.* I don't know if I'm right about this, though. I'm guessing, really.

Maybe she understands what I'm saying, because she stops talking.

Then Marc comes in and fills the silence. "Who's excited for fifth grade?!" he says, clapping his hands. "I know I am! And Chester is, too!"

He touches Gus's shoulder, which we all know is a mistake. Gus doesn't like to be touched at all unless he's in control of the touching, like when he gives someone else a hug. This doesn't happen very often, but I've seen it a few times. He will hug his mother or father from behind and they're always surprised. "Thank you for the hug!" they'll say. He's never done this to me. I think he's still scared I'll touch him accidentally.

Now even though Gus flinches because he doesn't like to be touched, Marc leaves his hand there. I don't know why Marc does this on a morning when everyone is already nervous enough. I worry that Gus might explode from too much touching, but he surprises me: He bends his head so his cheek touches his dad's hand. He leaves it there for a few seconds.

That's nice, I say. *Letting your dad touch your shoulder.*

I wish he could hear me. I wish he could know how doing

this helps us all feel better. I remember when I thought Penny could understand what I said and I talked to her all the time because it *seemed* like she was listening, but of course she wasn't. She loved me, I knew, but she could never hear me.

Which is why I can't believe my ears when I hear Gus say, *I know.*

He hasn't moved his lips, but I hear him say it anyway. It's a simple, clear boy's voice that I've never heard him actually use. When they come, his words are mostly high and squeaky and hard on the ears. Sara keeps a count of the words he uses, but I'm not sure why because I've never heard him say any words that mean anything.

Until now.

I scoot closer to his chair, though I'm careful not to touch any part of his body because I know he has to concentrate on letting his dad's hand sit on his shoulder like that.

It's nice of you letting him touch you this morning. He's nervous, too. We all are. I'm saying too much, maybe. I can't help it though. I feel anxious like a puppy again, with everything going on.

I said I know. I'm trying.

I watch him carefully. His eyes are closed and his lips haven't moved. I don't know how he just did that. I know he talked, though. I heard him. I know it was Gus because he sounded like he was tired of being the center of attention. Like he loves his parents but he wants to get this day *over with*.

I know how he feels because I feel the same way. I'm nervous too, even though I found out this morning I don't have to stay the whole time today. I just have to walk inside so all the kids can meet me. Then Ms. Winger, the teacher, will tell us when I can start coming to school.

Gus doesn't say any more to me for the rest of breakfast, which is okay. It was very exciting to talk to each other but I'm not going to push it or ask him a lot of questions about why he rocks or drones or likes sparkly pens so much.

Even though I'm not staying at school, Sara thinks it's a good idea for me to wear my old blue service-dog-in-training vest. Last night she and Marc had an argument about it.

"This way there won't be any questions. Everyone will understand he's a working dog."

"But his vest says 'In-Training,'" Marc said.

"That's okay. I've already explained all this and I promise no one will be reading what it says. The point is to have him look official."

"Won't people wonder why he's still wearing a training

vest a year from now?"

"No one will care because they'll love him so much!" Sara said, hugging me.

Marc lowered his voice. "You don't worry you're setting your sights a little high for all this? He's just a dog, after all. He'll be a novelty for a week and then it'll wear off and he'll be like every other person who hovers around Gus and tries to get him to look up."

Sara sat up. "Oh, don't say it like that, Marc!"

"I'm sorry," he said, laughing. "I'm kidding. I just think we do better when we go into things with low expectations."

I think Marc is right, but I also think it's too late. We're all too nervous and Sara has told us too many times how great fifth grade is going to be.

How to Get a Sparkly Pen

IN THE CAR RIDE TO SCHOOL, Gus rocks so hard in his seat, Sara tells him to stop or he might hurt me. I'm sitting in the backseat, as far away from him as possible because Gus doesn't like it when the car turns and my toenails accidentally slide into him. I'm trying to be ready for that and keep my toenails to myself.

He stops rocking for a second. *You won't hurt me,* I say.

He shakes his head like he wants to say, *I didn't think so.*

He doesn't say it, though. Or I don't hear it. He goes back to rocking, a little slower now.

"Chester's coming into school with us, do you remember that, Gus? You don't have to hold the leash but you can if you want."

It's raining a little, so we all listen to the squeak of wind-shield wipers.

"Do you think you want to do that? Do you want to hold Chester's leash so other kids will know he belongs to you?"

It's not a great idea, I say. *Not on the first day. One step at a time is better, I think.*

Maybe he hears me, because he says his version of no, which is "NIS! NIS! NIS!"

"Fine, Gus. It's okay. Thanks for using your words and telling me."

Gus is okay getting out of the car.

He's also okay walking toward the building. He looks like maybe he's forgotten where we're going even though he's wearing a new backpack and all new clothes. It's like he doesn't realize where he is until a little girl runs by fast and screams, "GIVE ME BACK MY PEN!" I can't help feel-ing scared at how loud a little girl's voice can be. Gus looks scared too. I know what he's probably thinking: *Pens aren't safe here—people take them.*

He stops walking right there.

"Come on, sweetheart," Sara says. "There's nothing to be afraid of. You remember all this. We're going into school. We're almost to the front door. We just have to get inside and then you'll remember everything."

Gus won't move. Sara tries walking with me a few steps ahead to see if he'll follow. He doesn't.

"Come on, Gus! We don't want to be late!"

Nothing.

Finally she walks back. "I need you to keep walking, Gus. I'm going to count to three."

Gus hates it when she counts to three.

"One . . . two . . ."

Usually this gets him moving, but this time instead of taking a step, Gus closes his eyes and puts his fingers in his ears. I'm pretty sure this means he won't move at all, even if his mom says three. I don't know what's going to happen, except right then, a woman walks out to us in the parking lot and says, "Hello. You must be Gus."

She has curly brown hair and wears lots of bracelets that slide down her arm and make a funny noise. She kneels down in front of him, right where his eyes are looking so he has to see her. "Hello, Gus. My name is Ms. Winger and I'm very happy to meet you."

He doesn't say anything of course, but he also doesn't look away. She stays very still so her jewelry doesn't move or make a noise.

"I heard that you like sparkly pens. I just happen to have a few in my desk for you to earn today when you get your work done. Do you want to come with me and see what they look like?"

He does. I can tell by the way he's holding his breath.

I wag my tail. *She's really nice! She knows about sparkly pens!*

When she stands back up, Gus's eyes go with her, which hardly ever happens. He doesn't like looking at people, but she's different. He likes looking at her bracelets, I think.

"First we have to walk into school. Are you ready to walk into school, Gus?"

Gus nods. I'm surprised. It's like he's answering her question. I've never seen him do that before.

She starts walking like she expects him to follow and he does. He walks faster than he was walking before. Sara looks at me and we both follow until we get to the front door and Ms. Winger turns around. "I'm sorry, Sara—I should have said this sooner. I've talked to the other fifth-grade teacher and we'd like to wait a week or so before we bring Chester into school."

Sara looks at me. "But Gus is expecting this. You agreed—"

Ms. Winger holds up her hand. "I *do* want to have Chester in the classroom, but not on the first day. I have to make sure I've got everyone's attention on me before I bring in a beautiful distraction like Chester. I'm sure he's a wonderful dog, I just want to wait."

I can tell Sara wants to say something more, but how can she when Ms. Winger seems magical and got Gus to walk from the parking lot to the front door?

"I'll let you know when we're ready to invite him in. Why don't you say goodbye to your mom and Chester, Gus, and we'll go inside and find those pens?"

Gus doesn't say goodbye of course, but he lets his mom hug him and turns back to the door like he wants to go in now.

Good for you! I say, trying to sound upbeat. *I hope you get a great pen!*

A second later they're gone.

For the rest of the morning, Sara has a hard time working at her computer and I have a hard time doing anything except watching Sara and worrying. At lunch, Marc comes home and sits down to the bowl of soup Sara has put out for him. "So tell me everything. How did it go?"

"I think she might be wonderful. She's bought sparkly pens for him to earn." Even though she's saying nice things, she isn't smiling. "I don't know. I get so mad when he has a bad teacher who doesn't make an effort or care about him, and then we get a nice one who does and I wonder if it's going to make any difference. Oh, Marc, I just keep thinking—"

She's sad, I can tell, which makes me go over and put my nose in her lap. "If he doesn't have a better time this year, we may have to send him to that out-of-district placement. He'll be three hours away and we won't see him all week! It breaks my heart to imagine." She takes a deep breath. "I just want this year to work out better."

"I know," Marc says. "I know."

"Is he ever going to appreciate this new teacher and how hard people are working to connect with him?"

Marc comes over and hugs her. "I don't know. But we'll appreciate her, right? Just like we appreciate Chester here."

All day long, I think about how Gus answered me this morning.

For so long I wished Penny could understand all the questions I wanted to ask her: *What if I can't do the job I'm given? What if I don't love the person I'm matched with as much as I love you?* After that terrible day on the farm, I wanted to tell her how sorry I was, and it wasn't her fault, but I couldn't.

Now I wonder if maybe I imagined hearing Gus talk. I can't wait for him to get home to test it out again.

After Sara brings him home, though, he's tired. Sara reads a note written in a blue book she pulls out of his backpack. "Gus was a little nervous today and chose not to participate in art class or circle meeting or any of the other class activities. We'll try again tomorrow."

I know this makes Sara sad.

I want to follow Gus into his room and ask, *What's wrong with circle meeting? Why don't you like art?* But he pushes me out the door of his room. Apparently hearing each other talk doesn't work through closed doors.

It also doesn't work if he's not in the mood.

At dinner I try again. *What's wrong with circle meeting?* I ask. *What's art again?*

Nothing.

I can't help feeling sad. For so long, I've wanted someone to talk to. Sure, there are other dogs in the neighborhood, but you'd be surprised how little grown dogs have in common with each other. When we're young, we play in a heap, hardly noticing our differences. As grown-ups, it's different. We meet on walks, attached to leashes, and we don't say anything. The closest we come to real communication is probably at night when we race outside for our last pee and activate the Neighborhood Emergency Alert System, where an emergency is any time one of us goes outside and it's dark out. Then we bark to let the others know we're outside and it's dark. Maybe I started this, I'm not sure. Maybe the dark makes me nervous because loud noises could come from anywhere, so I bark to scare them away. Then the other dogs start and I have to admit, I feel a little better. But it's not a real conversation and the truth is, it's lonely. They aren't real friends and I usually feel embarrassed when I see those dogs during the day.

I pretend to ignore them and keep moving so they won't sniff my rump. I know it's tempting and I'm tempted too, but the longer I live with Sara and Marc and Gus, the more aware I am of how important social interactions are.

I don't think Penny was very good at these. I know Gus is terrible. On the street, in the grocery store, Sara is always reminding him, "Be polite, Gus. Say hello." He says hello in a high-pitched, squeaky voice that's hard for people to understand and then he never says anything else.

I'm working hard to be polite and not smell rumps because I don't want Sara's life to be any harder than it already is. I'm here to help, even if we haven't figured out how I'll do that.

How Not to Help

GUS HAS A BAD NIGHT. INSTEAD of eating his dinner, he stares off into the distance. After dinner, I'm hoping he'll go to his window so we can check on the birds and their nest together, but even after I say, *I think the mother bird is sitting on some eggs,* he doesn't go.

Instead, he walks upstairs to his room and lies down on his bed.

Sara looks in a little later, then comes down to say, "It's six thirty and he's fast asleep with all his clothes on. I'm not sure what to do."

Marc isn't either. They decide to let him sleep for a while, which might be a mistake because when Sara wakes him up at eight to get his pajamas on, he cries louder than I've ever heard him cry. It makes my heart race and my legs shake. I run into the room to get it to stop.

Sara is sitting on the bed with him, but in the terrible confusion of screaming, I forget everything.

I forget that I should never touch him.

I forget that if I have to touch him, my nose is the worst thing to do it with.

I forget all of that and put my paws in his lap and lick his neck and his ears. The screaming gets worse and Gus shoves me, hard. I fly across the room and hit the bookshelf where they keep the few books Gus allows his parents to read to him.

Sara screams, "GUS, NO!"

I scramble out of the room as she starts to cry herself. "You mustn't ever hurt Chester!" Both of them crying at once is too much and I limp away.

How to Get Ready

———————— 🐾 ————————

I DON'T GO BACK TO SCHOOL THE next day. Or the next. Or the day after that.

Finally Ms. Winger sends a note home saying, "Chester may join us at school for an hour on Thursday."

The night before, I have a hard time sleeping. I try to imagine what this will be like. I've seen classrooms on TV, which are loud with children's voices and chairs scraping. I'm most afraid of what will happen if something goes wrong. If Gus panics, it's possible I'll panic too. I don't think Sara and Marc know what happened in the thunderstorm at the farm. They think of me as a smart dog who almost passed the service dog test but didn't quite.

They trust me to do this job and I want to prove I can.

I think about the birds building their nest. I can do this, I think. I can.

I wake up early in the morning and check the spot in the mudroom where my vest is laid out, along with my leash. I wait in the kitchen for hours, it seems like, for the others to wake up.

Two garbage trucks roll by and one recycling truck, but I don't bark at all. I have to stay concentrated. Today is the first real day of my first real job. I'm a working dog now, even if I don't have the same orange vest as my dog brothers.

I will still have duties and responsibilities.

I will do what I am told.

I won't be too sensitive or overreact.

When they finally wake up, I'm exhausted from waiting for this day to start.

School

MS. WINGER IS STANDING IN FRONT of the school, waiting for us. I listen carefully to her conversation with Sara. "Most of the kids are very excited to have Chester in class. A few of them have had some bad experiences with dogs, though, and they're a little nervous. For this first day, we'd like to introduce Chester and give kids a chance to say hello, but I don't want to push it or have him stay too long. Does that sound okay?"

"Fine," Sara says, but I can tell she's mad. "Just to remind you, though, he's meant to be here for Gus, helping Gus socialize and feel more comfortable around school. He's not here for the other kids. He's a service dog."

"He's a therapy dog, which is different. If the goal is helping Gus socialize with other children, then we need to make sure the other children are comfortable."

Now I feel even more scared. Sometimes when I get scared, I accidentally bark. I have to remember not to. Barking scares kids. Barking is only good for talking to other dogs in the neighborhood. At school there are no other dogs. Only me.

The classroom looks like classrooms I've seen on TV. All the children go quiet when we walk in. One girl points and says, "Oh, he's so cute!"

Gus wouldn't hold my leash out in the hallway, so Sara is holding it, walking us both up to the front of the room. Gus walks on his toes, flaps his hands, and makes squeaking noises.

Ms. Winger pulls out two chairs for Gus and Sara to sit down in. I sit next to Gus so kids will see us together even though it means my leash is stretched across his lap.

Ms. Winger says to the class, "Okay, Gus. Would you like to introduce your friend who's going to be joining us in class a few days a week?"

Gus doesn't say anything of course.

Sara leans in to his ear and whispers, "Gus, say, 'This is my dog, Chester.'"

Sara is smart to try this. The only time Gus talks out

loud is when he repeats the words someone else has given him.

This time, though, he doesn't say anything.

He pushes my leash off his lap so no part of me touches him.

Sara smiles at the group. "Hi, everyone, this is Chester. He's here to help Gus get more independent and better at talking with other kids. He's a very sweet dog, and Ms. Winger has said there will be certain times in the day when you'll be allowed to come over and visit with him if you've finished all your other work."

Sara's trying not to look nervous. She's better than Penny at this, but I can still tell.

"Are there any questions?"

A girl raises her hand. "What will he do for Gus?"

"That's a good question, Amelia," Ms. Winger says. "We're working that out. For now, he'll be here in the mornings, over in the special corner we've made for him. If Gus needs some chill-time, he'll take Chester with him. Gus has to remember that Chester will be waiting to hear his commands. The only person who's allowed to tell Chester what to do is Gus. Does everyone understand that? Chester shouldn't have eighteen voices telling him what to do. Only

Gus. Okay, everybody?"

I'm surprised hearing Ms. Winger say this rule. I've lived with Gus for a while now and so far he's never given me a command. I wonder if Ms. Winger knows this.

"Are there any more questions?"

One girl asks how old I am. Sara tells her about a year. Another boy asks where I'll go to the bathroom and if someone will have to clean it up if I go number two.

"We're going to take care of that, Wes, don't worry, okay?" Ms. Winger says.

A tall boy with curly hair sitting toward the back of the class raises his hand. This whole time he's been leaning back on two legs of his chair. He keeps almost falling and then he doesn't. "Yes, Ed?"

"It's kind of unfair that Gus gets to bring his dog in and the rest of us don't, isn't it?"

Sara shifts in her seat like she wants to answer this boy, but Ms. Winger holds up one hand as if to say, *Let me.* "Remember I explained this to everyone yesterday, Ed? Chester is a therapy dog. This means he has a job to do. The reason the rest of you can't bring your dogs to school is because you don't have specially trained dogs, and you don't need help navigating your day. Now—why don't we wrap this up by letting Gus show us some of the things Chester can do. I'll bet he has a few tricks, right?"

Ed's question made us both look down at the floor, but now Ms. Winger has made us feel better. Sara sits up straighter. So do I. "Oh yes, of course," Sara says. "He'd love to show you a few things he can do." She leans in to Gus's shoulder and whispers, "Do you remember what you say to get him to lie down?" She waits for a second. "Say, 'Chester, down.'"

I start to lie down but Sara stops me. "Not yet, Chess. Let Gus say it first."

I sit back up and look at Gus, who is staring at something out the window.

We all wait. For a long time.

"Gus?" Sara says hopefully.

"Can you ask Chester to lie down?" Ms. Winger says. I look at him again. *Can you say it, Gus? I'll do it if you say it. Or we can show them another trick.* Penny taught me a few that she called "silly party tricks," even though she never went to parties. One was "Chester, pray," where I put my paws together and bend my face into them. *If you put your hands together and pray, I'll do it too. Everyone always thinks that's funny.*

76

We wait.

We keep waiting. We wait for so long I wonder if Ms. Winger is doing this on purpose to show Sara that Gus doesn't really want me here.

I want to say: *But look at how much Sara wants me here.*

Gus smiles at something out the window. I lick his hand so he remembers that I'm here and everyone is watching. Finally Ms. Winger says, "Maybe we should let Gus's mom take Chester home now and everyone should say thank you to Sara and Gus for letting us meet Chester!" She claps loudly and a few kids join in.

I look around. *But we haven't done anything,* I think.

Then something happens. Gus's hands move together. He waits for a second so everyone is watching. Then, without a sound, he puts them together. He's doing what I told him to do! He's praying!

I lie down on the ground and put my paws together. Penny said it's even funnier if I put my nose under my paws, so I do that too.

Sara's the first one to realize what we've done. She laughs and claps. "Good job, Gussie! You showed them a trick! Look, everyone—Chester is praying!"

Now they understand and more kids clap.

Ms. Winger bends over me. "Oh my goodness, puppy, what are you praying for?" She's smiling, like what we've just done has changed her mind on a few things. Like she was only pretending to like me before but now she really does.

was listening in when Penny told me all this. Which means he understands so much more than we ever thought. He

How to Tell a Joke

"I'M TELLING YOU, MARC, GUS WASN'T even *in* the room when Penny showed me that trick." Sara's been smiling the whole time she's told Marc the story about our school visit today. "I *know* he wasn't. And I never showed him the trick because I would have assumed Gus doesn't understand what praying means. Obviously he does and the kids loved it! But how did Gus *know* Chester could do that?"

Marc thinks about it. "He was listening outside the door when Penny was here? Maybe he's more interested in Chess than we thought?"

"That's the only explanation that makes any sense! He was *listening* in when Penny told me all this. Which means he understands so much more than we ever thought! He understands a joke! He even had great timing—he waited until the last second when Ms. Winger had essentially said, 'Show's over' and then he pulled out the last act . . ."

Marc smiles and shakes his head. "And Gus really put his hands together?"

"Yes! With the whole class watching!"

I don't know if it would make a difference if I told her: *I don't think Gus overheard your conversation. I'm pretty sure he just heard me. We hear each other sometimes.*

Would that make her feel better or worse? I'm not sure.

How to Worry

THE NEXT MORNING, I ACCIDENTALLY EAT breakfast so quickly I forget to taste it. Then I sit by the front door and wait to go to school again with Gus. No one explains anything until Sara comes back for her cup of coffee and says, when she almost trips over me, "Oh, Chess, I'm sorry. You're not coming today. We're not going to school. Gus has a doctor's appointment in Hartford. Dogs can't come to doctor's offices."

I wish I could tell her I know all about doctor's offices! I can press door openers and stand back so they don't hit me! I can help with elevators!

I can't tell her this of course, so I wait at home alone all day, listening to the radio and mysterious stories interspersed with weather predictions that make me more and more anxious. "Heavy rain will make driving conditions difficult" is not what you want to hear, over and over, when all your people are in a car somewhere and you've had to pee since right after breakfast.

You don't want to listen to rain, or smell it, or hear car horns in the distance honking.

When Marc finally comes home, I'm happy until he says, "Hey, where are the others, Chess? They should be home by now."

That's also not what you want to hear. I don't go back to my bed because lying on the floor makes it easier for me to hear and feel when a car comes in.

I keep waiting for hours, it seems like. Finally Sara's car comes in. I smell them before the door even opens. I'm so relieved and happy, I dance around in circles dribbling pee, though Marc just let me out a little while ago. "Oh, sweet Chester," Sara says. "Were you worried? You shouldn't have worried. We just hit traffic coming home, that's all."

Marc hugs Sara and she tells him more. The doctor kept them waiting forever and ordered two tests they had to do then or else drive all the way back next week.

"Did they tell you anything?" Marc asked.

"We have to wait. For now we have periodic incontinence on top of everything else."

I don't know what incontinence means, but I wonder if it has anything to do with the way Gus smells like urine sometimes. It's a smell I love. It makes me follow him around and sit outside his bedroom just to enjoy that cloudy aroma.

"I told the doctor it's happened four times in the last month and it doesn't seem related to stress. He's checking urinary tract infections and some other things. Kidney stones, bladder function."

I only understand that something new and worrying is happening with Gus. I go and stand near him. He doesn't have his wonderful urine smell now, but it's okay.

"This is what always happens, isn't it?" Sara says to Marc, though she's looking at both of us. "We have one great day that feels like everything's changed and then the next it feels like nothing has."

Non-Breakthroughs

IT'S MONDAY WHEN I FINALLY GET to go back to
school. Sara tells Gus, "Chester will only be there for two
hours. He won't stay the whole day. We're doing this a little
bit at a time, so everyone can adjust."

It's not me Sara's worried about. She ruffles my ears and
touches my nose and whispers into the top of my head,
"You're a good dog, aren't you?"

She's worried about Gus. This morning he woke up with
that wonderful smell all over his bed. It made her sad, so I
sat near her while she changed the sheets.

I don't mind the smell, I try to tell Gus. *In fact I like it.* But
he either isn't listening or can't hear me. It's hard for me
to predict what he hears and what he doesn't. Maybe he's

answering and I can't hear him.

Ever since our joke at school, we haven't talked to each other at all. I tried to tell him, *Good job telling me to pray at school. You made your mom really happy.*

He didn't answer me or else I couldn't hear him.

I'm starting to think I know how Sara feels: It's sad to have something feel like a breakthrough and then maybe it isn't.

Ms. Palmer

🐾

I'M SURPRISED. IT TURNS OUT THAT you can learn a lot going to school.

For instance, I learn the reason Ms. Winger waited for so long before letting me come to school wasn't because of any kids in the class, it was because of Ms. Palmer next door, the other fifth-grade teacher who sometimes says, loud enough for me to hear, that she doesn't believe in therapy dogs. Most of Ms. Winger's class goes over to her room for math, but I never go because she says no dogs are allowed in her class.

I overheard her talking to Ms. Winger. "I can't control what you do, Marianne, but no, that dog isn't coming into my classroom. He's a distraction, that's all. There isn't any real work he's doing."

Even though Ms. Winger said, "Okay, that's fine. I'll keep him here with me then," Ms. Palmer wanted to keep talking about it: "It's like all that 'Read to a Dog' nonsense. You want kids to practice reading out loud to someone who won't interrupt, give them a stuffed animal. But a dog who isn't listening and is only going to get up and walk away? No, thank you."

I remember Penny taking me to a few library sessions of "Read to a Dog." I loved those stories. I never wanted to get up and walk away. If I could talk to Ms. Palmer, I'd tell her *not enough* people read to their dogs. I have a feeling that if I'd had more stories read to me, I'd understand more about the humans I love.

Some subjects, like math, are too hard for me to understand, and other subjects, like the story of Christopher Columbus, aren't. Apparently most people think Christopher Columbus discovered America, but he didn't really. There were a lot of people who already lived here. He just walked in and said, "I'll take this," and he did.

I'm also learning the days of the week and months of the year. As a dog you hear these names all the time, but no one ever explains them. Fifth graders know the calendar already but they're tracking the moon cycle every night on the calendar. I already know all about the moon, but now I understand what yesterday means and tomorrow. Before, I thought those were names of days and I never understood why they happened so often.

At school, it's easy to see how different Gus is from other kids his age. Other kids talk to each other in the hall before school starts. In class, after the bell rings, they use their faces to make jokes. They widen their eyes or blow out their cheeks and crack each other up. I don't understand most of it. All I know is that Gus can't do any of this. At school he never laughs at what the other kids are doing. Instead, he laughs at things going on inside his head.

At recess, I stay with Gus as much as possible, but if he's earned time with his sparkly pen, he won't do anything except sit on a bench and wiggle his pen back and forth, fast, in the corner of his eye. If I talk to him, he doesn't hear me, or at least he doesn't answer.

Why do you wiggle your pen so much? I say.

Nothing.

Maybe you should play with other kids a little.

Nothing.

It's like he goes into a trance with his pen. He can't see or hear anything when he's got his pen.

Mama

— ❖ —

FOR A WHILE I THOUGHT SARA was right, that Gus didn't have anything at school he liked very much. School makes him so nervous he walks on his toes, with his legs really straight wherever he goes, the same way he walked around me in the beginning. Walking like this means he doesn't look where he's going. Usually he doesn't bump into anything because everyone sees him coming and gets out of his way. If they don't see him, I nudge his leg with my nose, which makes him stop. Then he waits for a while before he starts walking again.

Sometimes he walks so slowly, his teacher's aide, Ms. Cooper, has to say, "Come on, Gus, we need to keep going." Ms. Cooper is younger than the other teachers. Sometimes

I think she's scared that if she says the wrong thing, Gus might have a tantrum, so she never pushes him too hard or makes him walk too fast.

I'm pretty sure Gus walks like this because he doesn't like that he's going to Ms. Cunningham's room for speech therapy, or Ms. Watusik's room for occupational therapy, or Mr. Foster in the gym to practice catching a ball. Gus can't do most of the things they're trying to teach him. In OT he practices handwriting, which he hates. In speech therapy he practices using a talking computer, which has a voice he can't stand. He covers his ears every time it speaks. Ms. Cunningham hasn't noticed, but I have. And what does it matter if Gus can catch a ball? He'll never do it again after he learns. I'm not surprised that he walks slowly to all these places. It means he has to spend less time once he gets there, which is smart of him.

There's one place that isn't like this for Gus. He doesn't have to be told to keep walking or hurry up. His legs never stiffen up on his way there.

That place is the cafeteria, but he doesn't love it for the reason that I do: because of the smells and the food that sometimes falls on the floor between my paws.

Gus loves the corner behind the trash cans, where people

are supposed to sort the things on their trays into compost and trash. In that corner there's a magic rolling mat that carries trays through a window. I can't see the mat, but that's how I heard Gus describe it in his mind. Sometimes I hear his thoughts even if he's not talking to me. He's saying it loud enough in his mind for me to hear, I guess.

Magic rolling mat! Bye-bye, tray!

I can see the tray move and then disappear. It's a good trick. If I was younger and not trained, I might even bark at it because it scares me a little, seeing things disappear.

But that's not Gus's favorite part.

His favorite part is when the face of a woman, brown like me, with silver hair, peeks through the black plastic ribbons and smiles at him. Every day she smiles and says the same thing: "How's my boy?"

She has a beautiful smile even though she doesn't have as many teeth as most people do.

"You come on back here now and say hello to me."

She always waves and he always walks around the corner to the doorway of a room where she stands and waits for him. Her name is Mama and she wears a white apron over a long, brightly colored dress.

"You stand right here and keep me company," she says.

Her voice has an accent because she's from Jamaica, she told Gus once. That's why she doesn't mind the heat of this job or the steam either. "Reminds me of home!" she says.

I don't know if she can hear Gus talk to her the way I can. At first I thought she must, because she answers the questions I know he'd ask. "I can't put this tray in yet. I need to fill it with more glasses," she'll say.

Or "Almost ready with silverware. Not quite."

Gus loves these updates. He loves her machine with its steam and all the buttons and hissing sounds. He'd like her to show him exactly how it all works, but he doesn't know how to ask her out loud. Still, she understands and shows him parts of it. "This button here, that starts the dryer," she'll say.

Gus loves the machine and the steam and the trays on the rolling mat, but mostly, I think, he loves Mama. She's the only adult in the school that I've heard him talk to on his own. I've only heard him say a few words to her, but that's more than he says to anyone else, unless he has to for a sticker on his reward star chart.

It's sometimes hard to hear, but I know he's said, "Hello, Mamá!" at least once. I know he also said, "Dog," and touched the top of my head.

Another thing I've noticed is that Ms. Cooper never sees any of this. She stands in the hall while Gus comes in here, but she never watches what's happening. Usually she uses this as a chance to look at her phone. Sometimes I think Ms. Cooper is more interested in her phone than she is in Gus. She's definitely not as interested in Gus as I am because she's doesn't see the way Gus and Mama talk to each other with their eyes and their smiles. She's never noticed that Gus *does* have something he loves at school.

I wish I could tell Sara.

I wish Sara could see the way Mama and Gus smile at each other. I wish she knew that Gus once said hello and introduced me. He never gets stickers or stars for doing any of that. He gets smiles from Mama, which is all he wants.

I know it would be a relief to Sara if she knew this because it's not just some*thing* he loves. It's some*one*.

Fright Fest

❖

ON SATURDAY, SARA GETS GUS UP early. When he's sitting at the table for breakfast, she says, "Today's the day, Gussie! We're going back to Fright Fest!"

This surprises me. *Fright Fest?* I think.

Obviously Gus understands what she's saying and he's excited. He rocks back and forth in his chair so much, he almost falls over.

He doesn't notice when I say, *Fright Fest? What's that?*

Sara doesn't help. She keeps smiling and saying, "Remember last year when you walked right up to that zombie holding an ax?"

More rocking and a squeal from Gus.

A zombie holding an ax? I say. I want someone to explain this to me.

"Remember the lady who got her head chopped off?" Sara laughs as if this is all very funny.

Gus laughs too.

"I was thinking we should bring Chester with us this time. That way we don't have to worry about you getting lost in the crowd, right, Gus?"

Me? I think. *Walking around with zombies and headless women?*

Even Marc isn't sure. "You want to bring Chester to Fright Fest?"

"Why not? If Gus loves it, why shouldn't Chester? Plus, Chester's been trained for this. If Gus holds his leash, he can't wander too far without Chester sitting down and waiting for us to catch up."

I look over at Gus. I can tell he's excited. If his chair was a rocket he'd push the blast-off button right now.

Sara leans closer and whispers to Marc, "He loves it so much, Marc, remember?"

In the car, I can't help myself, I keep asking Gus questions: *What's a zombie? What happens to the woman without her head?* He doesn't answer, but he laughs and imitates the sounds zombies must make. I don't know if it's the right sound because I've never met a zombie, I've only heard people talk about them on TV.

Just hearing people talk about them, though, was scary enough for me.

Marc is driving, so Sara turns around and explains it all to me the way she does sometimes. I think it's her way of reminding Gus what to expect. "It's a regular amusement park, Chess, with roller coasters and bad food, but for the month of October every Saturday, they have people dress up like ghosts and ghouls and walk around scaring people."

Did she say food? I ask Gus.

Halo! Gus says, but not out loud.

I don't understand. He laughs and rocks, more excited than I've ever seen him.

Sara says, "They also have this thing where you can ask at Guest Services for a light stick halo if you don't want the people to scare you. Do you remember that, Gus? We got one for you and then you kept taking it off because you *wanted* those people to get closer to you?"

He remembers. He's giggling, but I can hear him. *I remember! I remember!*

They must be funny! I say to Gus. *It must be okay!*

Yes, they're so funny, Gus says. *You'll laugh, Chester, I know you will.*

He's forgotten dogs don't laugh. We do other things like jump around and lick hands, which is what I do now because it's the first time he's ever used my name.

It's so great, he says. *So, so great.*

How to Say Yes

IT TURNS OUT THAT ZOMBIES ARE people who look like they're bleeding but don't smell that way. They also look very dirty without smelling nice the way a dirt-covered person should. And they growl a lot.

At first I don't even realize these are the zombies because they seem like a bunch of people acting like mean dogs. Thank goodness I remember my training well enough not to growl back. Then I watch Gus do something funny every time he sees one of them. He crosses his arms and karate chops the air in front of him. It makes him laugh so instead of feeling nervous he feels powerful, I think. It also means none of the zombies come too close to us, so even if he's not fighting anyone, he is keeping them away.

After we get past three of them, I feel a lot braver and I can tell Gus does, too. It's kind of fun watching him make karate chop X's, and we spend most of the morning looking for zombies for him to have imaginary fights with. If Gus wants to go on a ride, Marc rides with him and I sit with Sara, who scratches my neck and tells me what a good job I'm doing.

Those are the only times I eat food off the ground. Otherwise I ignore the food—and believe me, there's a lot of food I have to ignore. For lunch I lie down under Gus's feet and watch two pigeons fight over a pizza crust. I try telling them they should share, but they either don't understand me or else they aren't listening.

After lunch, we wait for a long time for Gus to go on a ride with cars that kids can drive around a track. It seems like it's mostly for little kids. Still, when it's finally Gus's turn, he can't figure out how to make the car go. He starts to cry, so Marc gets into the car and drives for him so other kids won't have to watch a bigger boy cry. I was pretty sure we'd go home after that, but instead of leaving, Sara says, "Look, you guys. The Spooky Walk starts at five. Do you want to go for a walk through the woods and see some spooky people, Gus?"

No thank you! I say.

"Do you remember you were too scared to do it last year, but maybe this year you're big enough to try? Supposedly it has a fog machine and witches along the way."

Really, that doesn't sound like a good idea to me, I say. Unfortunately, no one is listening to me, including Gus.

He stops walking. He looks at his mom. *Fog machine?* he says, but not out loud.

Sara smiles like it's great that he's thinking about this.

"I don't think it'll be super scary. I think it's more like a walk through the woods where spirits and fairies come out from behind trees. It's more magical scary than scary scary."

I don't think Gus is thinking about that, he's thinking about the fog machine. Mama once called her dishwasher at school a fog machine when she opened it up and a big cloud came out. Gus thinks there's going to be a dishwasher in the woods.

Even I know there won't be. Woods don't have dishwashers.

No fog machine! I say.

He doesn't hear me. Or if he hears, he's not listening.

Instead he's rocking and smiling and clicking his tongue.

"You want to go?" Sara says, smiling even more. "I think he wants to go, Marc."

Gus bounces a little and squeaks at a boy walking by with a lot of glow sticks around his neck. It's starting to get dark, which means his head looks like an egg in a glowing nest.

"Let's do it, Marc. I think we should do it."

"I don't know, Sare. I feel like we've had a great day, maybe we shouldn't push it." He's thinking about Gus crying on the cars a few minutes ago. Sara doesn't like it when Marc says things like "Let's be careful." Or "No."

"Or maybe we build on a great day and do something bold because we shouldn't be afraid all the time."

Gus covers one ear with his hand, like he's not sure if he wants to hear this conversation or not. He rocks back and forth, which is what he usually does when he listens, even though to other people it doesn't look like he's listening.

"Okay," Marc says. "Let's give it a try . . ."

Gus squeaks and turns in the direction of the Spooky Walk like he's not only been listening the whole time, he's memorized this whole park and remembers where it is.

Unfortunately, the Spooky Walk has the longest line in the park. For most of the day, Gus has had a special card that the person at the front of the line stamps with a time, which means Gus has to wait the same amount of time as everyone else but he doesn't have to stand in line while he's waiting.

I don't think Gus can stand in lines.

He needs to walk back and forth and bounce up and down. If he had to stand in line, he would crash into people and make them mad.

"Uh-oh," Marc says after he asks the man up front to stamp our card. "He says that because this is a special event for Fright Fest, they can't give us a time to come back for this one, Gussie. We'd have to wait in line, which is about an hour right now. Looks like we can't do it."

The problem is Gus can see the first part. There's a forest and they've hung a curtain between two trees that you have to walk through. Every time the curtain moves, we can see a flash of green light.

Gus wants to see what that green light is.

I want to see what that green light is, too. It winks on and off when the curtain moves.

"I'm sorry about the Spooky Walk, Gus, but we should get going anyway," Marc says. "It'll be dark soon."

Gus doesn't want to leave. I can tell by the way his body has stopped moving.

"Dad's probably right, sweetheart," Sara says. "We don't

want to be here in the dark when it gets even scarier."

They start to walk away but Gus doesn't move.

"Come on, Gus," Marc calls. "It's time to go."

I want to help him. *Can you say nis, Gus? If you say nis they'll know you don't want to leave yet.*

He turns away from me like he can hear me but I'm confusing him. He already has too many voices talking to him. Sara bends down to look in his eyes. "What is it, babe? Do you want to stay and go on the Spooky Walk even if it means waiting in line? I think he wants to stay, Marc. Do you want to stay, Gus?"

Gus doesn't have a word for yes exactly. Usually his body says yes by squeaking and rocking. Sometimes his hands say it by flapping.

He doesn't do any of that now. He's scared that if he moves, they'll take him back to the car.

Say yes, I tell him with my mind. My eyes have an easier time finding his because he's almost always looking down. *Say yes and they'll stay. They'll let you see what the green light behind the curtain is.*

We all wait. That's one important thing about Gus. You have to be patient and wait for him to click through everything his brain is thinking.

I don't know what his brain is thinking right now. I can't hear him think.

Then I'm surprised.

"Y-y-y-" he starts to say. This is different from anything I've heard from Gus.

He wants this enough to force his mouth to say it.

"Yesss . . . ," he says and hiccups.

Sara puts her hand over her mouth. Marc hugs her from the side.

They want to hug Gus, I can tell, but they can't.

"Okay, buddy," Marc says. "Okay—you said yes, you want to stay. That means we're going to stay. We're definitely going to stay."

Spooky Walk

✦

IT'S NOT EASY. THEY TAKE TURNS waiting in line, while the other one waits with Gus and me on a bench beside the line. When it's finally our turn, Sara says she wants us to all go in together. Marc looks at her funny and she says, "Of course it's okay to bring Chester. It's the *woods*." She's already asked the guy up front, who looked at my vest and shrugged okay.

When we walk past the curtain, we hear an eerie howl that hurts my ears. I wish I could have said *nis* to this idea.

The green flashing light is bright and coming from inside a pot that a witch is stirring. "Are you *sure* you want to come in here?" she cackles. "The last people just disappeared. I think they've gotten *lost* in the woods."

Sara laughs and whispers to Gus, "She probably says that to everyone."

Say nis, I tell him. *Say you've changed your mind and you've decided nis to the Spooky Walk.*

The witch has on a long black dress and running shoes underneath. I don't think the others can see her shoes, but I can. It worries me that maybe she's planning to run after us.

"If you don't see them, you might try looking for my cat, Brunhilda, or my Flying Monkeys. They escaped a while ago and they're getting pretty hungry by now."

Flying Monkeys?

"She's kidding," Sara says, and moves us along. She and Marc are holding Gus's hands, which surprises me. I've never seen him hold their hands before. It's nice to see, but then I wonder: *Wait, who's holding my leash?*

We leave the witch and walk up the path toward another light, this one white. We can hear noises in the woods around us but we can't see anything.

"Remember, these are all actors, so we don't have to be scared," Sara says, sounding scared. "They can say whatever they'd like, but no one's allowed to touch us."

Marc laughs a little. "Is that in a rule book somewhere?"

Just then a man wrapped in bandages jumps out from behind a tree in front of us. "Gahhhh!" he says, and then behind him, there's another voice. "Not them!"

The bandaged man steps back and disappears.

Sara whispers to Marc, "I think they see Chester and they know they shouldn't scare us too much. Isn't that nice of them?"

Yes, I think, *very nice,* and then a second later, a tree in the path ahead of us moves. It starts walking toward us, which makes me think maybe it's not a real tree at all. As soon as it gets closer, I know it's not a real tree because it smells like cigarettes.

"Watch out for the tree!" Marc says, pulling us to one side.

The tree runs by after we get out of its way. I don't know if Gus is as scared as I am. He's not making any noises, so it's hard to tell.

"Look, we're okay!" Sara is still trying to laugh, like this is all fun. This isn't fun. This stopped being fun when the tree started running. "There's a tunnel up ahead."

The tunnel is made out of sheets and has lights on inside, which seems fine until we walk in and there's so much fog that I start sneezing. I sneeze and sneeze and sneeze. When I finally stop, I can't see Gus or Sara or Marc. I walk ahead where they must have gone, but they aren't there.

That's when I remember that no one is holding my leash.

I'm all alone and I can't see anyone from my family. Even worse, I can't smell them. All I can smell is smoke and chemicals that hurt my nose.

I turn around to walk out the way we came in. If Gus isn't holding my leash, I'm scared he's lost. I need to find him. My heart starts racing faster.

Outside in the fresh air, I can breathe again, but my nose realizes right away they're not out here. They haven't come this way. My people are in the fog where my nose can't find them.

I go back in.

I bump into someone, who screams and says, "Something touched me!"

I don't want to scare other people. I just want to find my family. I keep my nose close to the ground but I still can't smell them. I listen carefully. I don't hear them, either.

I don't know why they aren't calling my name or looking for me.

I keep going through the tunnel, following a pair of men's shoes even though they don't belong to Marc. I need to get to the other end of this fog tunnel. *If I get there,* I think, *I will find them waiting for me.*

I pass another witch talking to a skeleton with red lights where his eyes should be.

I'm not going to look up again until I'm out of this tunnel.

I can smell fresh air. I'm getting closer.

I'm almost there. I listen for my name.

They'll be there and they'll be so happy to see me. They'll say, "Chester, what *happened,* are you okay?"

I keep walking. *Gus is okay,* I think. *Gus is with his parents and he is fine.* I can smell the air now. I follow the shoes out of the tunnel and that's when I realize my terrible mistake.

The shoes belong to a teenager and the spooky people in the forest don't mind scaring teenagers.

Someone jumps in front of us. "Gahh!"

A machine in his hand roars to life. I know it's a chainsaw because I got scared of one cutting down a tree in Penny's neighbor's yard. But this person isn't cutting down trees. This person is cutting down people.

I run away as fast as I can. I don't stop running because the chainsaw guy is running too.

Lots of people are running and laughing like this is funny but it's not funny. I run farther than anyone until my leash gets caught on something and I lurch back. I'm stuck. I have no choice. I have to scramble under the nearest bush I can find.

Behind me someone is yelling, "There's no chain in his chainsaw!"

A woman is laughing. "Don't be stupid, you guys. Come back!"

I don't know who she's calling stupid but I'm never going back. Never. I can't. My legs won't move now. I'm safe and hidden here.

I wait for a while and then I remember Gus. What if he's alone somewhere in these woods with this crazy chainsaw running around?

I hear Penny's voice in my head. *When loud noises happen, your person will need you. They have to be able to find you afterward.* Now my heart is really beating.

Gus is somewhere. Gus needs me.

It's dark out now. Very dark. He might have dropped my leash, but I'm the one who lost him. I have to leave my safe spot. I have to go back out there and find him.

I'm hiding so well, so deep in the bushes that it's hard to get out. When I finally do, I realize something terrible: My leash is tangled in the bushes. I try walking one way and then another. The bush won't let me go. I pull hard until my neck hurts. I look back and see the white tunnel of fog is far away.

The chainsaw starts up and it doesn't scare me because I have something to be more scared of now. I'm stuck in some bushes, far away in the woods where no one can find me.

Gus might be lost, but I'm even more lost.

The chainsaw man waiting outside the fog tunnel has chased at least four different groups coming out, maybe more. From here, he doesn't look so scary because I'm so far away. From here, the people look silly to be so surprised and scream so loud. I start to understand why Gus likes coming here. Feeling scared is fun if you know you're going to be all right afterward.

Except it's different out here where no one can see me or hear me barking. I don't know if anyone will ever find me. This is scary in a whole different way. They might look for me for a while and then give up. They might think I ran away for good, which happened in a movie I watched once with Penny. A dog and a cat ran away together and survived for a whole winter, catching their food and curling up together at night for warmth. If no one finds me, I'll be stuck here all winter long, with no cat friend to sleep with and no way to eat unless something dies in front of me. I'm really crying now. Barking and crying.

More people come out of the tunnel. More screams. More fog. More buzzing chainsaw. So loud that no one can possibly hear me.

I hear only myself and then, out of nowhere—I can't believe it!—there's a hand on my back.

There's a smell I love all around me. There's a crazy word I've heard him use once before when he was looking out his window. "GIT! GIT!"

It's Gus, and he's touching me with both of his hands like he was just as scared as I was, and now leashes aren't good enough, he wants to hold my fur.

In the distance, I hear Marc. "Sara! Over here! I think Gus found him!"

I hear their steps.

They're both far away. They've been out here looking for me. Combing through the woods. My family! My people!

Sara's voice gets closer. "*Gus* found him?" She's breathless from racing around in the dark. She can hardly believe it.

None of us can.

"Yes." Marc laughs, next to us now, petting me too. "Yes!"

Sara forgets the rule and hugs Gus hard. "Oh, baby, you *found him*. How did you *do* it?"

How to Find a Dog

THIS IS THE QUESTION EVERYONE KEEPS asking: How did Gus find me?

Over breakfast the next day, Marc shakes his head. "I still don't get it. It was so loud out there, with the chainsaw and everyone screaming, we couldn't even hear each other, so how'd he do it?"

"It's more evidence for my theory," Sara says. She's standing at the sink, drinking from her mug.

"What theory is that?"

"I think these two have a special connection."

Marc smiles, then raises his eyebrows. I'm learning to read people's faces better. This one means: *I don't think so.*

"I'm not kidding," Sara says, because she can understand

what his face is saying too. "Think about it, Marc. Gus keeps surprising us in lots of ways. Like when he told Chester to pray in front of the class. But in other ways too. The way he was so much braver yesterday than the year before. Why do you think that is?"

"Because he's getting older?"

"Right, but I think there's something else going on. He's *taking in* more of the world around him. He's more aware of things. We used to think he just lived in his own world, and that isn't really true anymore."

Marc's eyebrows are still up in the middle of his forehead. "Yeah—maybe a little. But I don't know if we can say that's Chester's doing, Sare."

"I think they communicate with each other. In some way the rest of us don't understand."

"Sara—"

"I *do*, Marc. Why do you always roll your eyes at my ideas?"

"I'm not rolling my eyes. I think we found a sweet dog and Gus is learning to tolerate him better, which is great. It means eventually maybe he'll start tolerating more new things in his life. But that doesn't make him Dr. Doolittle."

Who's Dr. Doolittle? I ask Gus.

He doesn't answer.

This has been the only sad part about everything that happened yesterday. After we were all so happy and relieved to have found each other, Gus didn't say anything the whole way home.

After Sara helped him get undressed and into bed, I stayed in his room, hidden in the corner so she wouldn't see me and call me back downstairs.

How did you find me? I whispered in the dark. *How did you do it?*

I know his sense of smell isn't as good as mine—no human can smell the way a dog can—but maybe he has a different sense that works better. Hearing, maybe? Or seeing in the dark. I wanted to know.

Can you tell me, Gus? Maybe it means you're really good at something and no one knows it yet. Maybe you have a special talent for hearing a dog cry even if there's a chain saw nearby.

Nothing.

Gus? I said again. *Do you want me to let you go to sleep?*

He did—I could tell from his grunt into his pillow. *Well, thank you for saving my life,* I said and left the room.

Quiet Mouth

ALL DAY, GUS SEEMS JUMPIER AT school. He can't stop making his clicking noises. Ms. Cooper touches his shoulder and whispers "Quiet mouth," which stops him for a little while, but not too long. Today she's saying "Quiet mouth" all day long until he's rocking and chewing on his shirt collar and then she starts saying "Quiet body," too.

On the walk to Ms. Watusik's office, he stops halfway there and starts crying, though it doesn't look like he's hurt. I nudge his leg with my nose and put my face between his knees. Eventually he keeps walking, but still I don't know what is wrong.

The only place he seems okay all day is at lunch in the cafeteria visiting Mama.

"How's my boy? You have a fun weekend?" she asks him. Mama always asks him questions like this, like she's never noticed that he doesn't answer. I look at him to see if he'll say something this time. I want him to tell his friend a story—to say, "Fright Fest," or "Dog lost." With Mama, that's all it would take. She'd understand the rest, I think.

She'd say, "Oh, you poor babe," looking at him, not at me.

That's another thing I like about Mama. She hardly notices me. Whenever we come back here, she looks only at Gus. I want him to say something so I can understand what's going on today and why he's so distracted and mad.

He doesn't.

Eventually, Mama starts humming one of her songs and says, "You better get going back to your class. You don't want to be late."

Gus doesn't move.

He bounces up and down on her spongy black mat. He's done this before, but today is different. He wants to tell her something, I can tell.

He doesn't want to leave until he gets it out.

Except then Ms. Cooper calls from the doorway. "Come on, Gus, it's class time."

She's behind him, so she can't see how he's about to

117

explode. She doesn't know how much Gus loves standing here with Mama.

"We've got three seconds, Gus, do you want me to count?"

No, I think. I see his hands curl up into fists. He hits his leg, hard, with one of them.

"One . . ."

I don't understand Ms. Cooper. She's counting but also looking at her phone. She doesn't see what's happening.

"Two . . ."

"I don't think so, sweetheart," Mama says. "Not in my dish room. No counting like that in Mama's dish room."

Ms. Cooper looks up, surprised. I don't think a dishwashing person is supposed to tell a teacher person what to do.

Mama nods at Gus with one of her big smiles, where you can see that she's missing a lot of teeth. "You're okay, sweetheart. You go on now and come back tomorrow. You tell me about your weekend then."

Gus takes one step back and then another. I can't get over it. I wonder how Mama knows that Gus hates when people count to three. I wonder if Mama hears what he's thinking the same way I do, or maybe even better than I do.

A Surprise

SARA PICKS ME UP EARLY FROM school, right after lunch. When we get in the car she says I have a surprise waiting for me at home.

A surprise? For me?

Recently, she bought a new brand of treats that I don't like as much as my old ones. I don't know if she's noticed that I shake my paw less enthusiastically for these treats than I did for my old ones. But maybe she has! Maybe we understand each other better than I thought!

You bought my old treats? I say. But no.

It's a different surprise. We walk inside the house, and sitting on the sofa with her hands folded over her knees is Penny! I bounce all around until she sits down on the floor and I can slip into her lap. She hugs my neck and kisses me and says she's so happy to see me.

"We had a little bit of a scare over the weekend," Sara says and tells Penny the whole story—of the Spooky Walk and the fog tunnel and getting lost in the woods.

I look at Penny's face. She doesn't like this story. It makes her nervous, like maybe I'm living with people who don't keep track of me.

Then Sara tells the happy ending: "It was Gus who found him! Gus! In the dark with so much noise and confusion and zombies running around. Even Marc and I were a little disoriented, but Gus wasn't. We still don't know how he did it."

I can tell that to Penny, this isn't a story with a happy ending. I lick her hand. I'm worried that she's going to get mad at Sara and tell her I should never go on any Spooky Walks again. I want to tell her it's good that I went! Gus and I learned a lot about each other! I have to do scary things if I want to help Gus!

Then Penny surprises me. She doesn't say anything about Sara's story. Instead she says, "That's fine, but I wanted to find out how you're doing on Chester's reading program. I've had time to do more research, and I've got some new materials for you."

Penny picks up a tote bag beside her filled with what look like books and flash cards.

Sara looks surprised too. "Oh, Penny, I'm sorry. I have to be honest and tell you we haven't done anything with Chester's reading program. We've been focusing on Gus, who's having a hard time in school right now. Chester is helping with that."

Penny looks confused. "Is he going to school with Gus?"

"Just a few hours a day as a therapy dog. He's there to help Gus interact with other children."

"I don't understand. He's not certified for that."

"He doesn't have to be. He mostly sits with Gus in the classroom and cafeteria as a way to encourage other kids to get to know Gus."

"So he's not home with you during the day? He doesn't have time to work on flash cards?"

"That's right." Sara smiles, grateful that Penny seems to understand. "He's gone most of the day and after dinner, we usually have family time. We wouldn't want to work him at night after he's spent most of his day working."

"But you just said, he's mostly sitting at school. He's not really working."

I know Penny is worried that I'm wasting my talents and all her training. I move closer and lick her hand again. I put my chin on her knee. *I do more than that.* I try to tell her, *It's important what I do. Gus has people he's almost friends with at school. I'm helping him with that.*

"Maybe you thought that teaching a dog to read was a silly parlor trick."

"No, Penny, it's not that—"

"It's not, though. It really isn't. Scientists are saying this might be our best chance to achieve real communication with animals. They've spent decades teaching sign language to gorillas and it's only worked in a few cases because apes don't inherently care about humans that much. Dogs do. Dogs care more about their relationships with people than any other animal does. They'd do anything to be able to talk to us."

"I understand that, Penny, but—"

"A dog like Chester doesn't come along very often. Some people would say you only find a dog as intelligent as Chester once in a lifetime. If he *could* learn to read, books would be written about him. I believe it's possible and people I've spoken to think it's possible too—"

Sara is tired, I can tell. It's been a long, confusing week full of breakthroughs and breakdowns. "We're trying to teach our son to speak, Penny. We want to know what he's thinking. We love Chester very much, and feel like he's part of our family now, but do we want to put all our effort into teaching him to read and talk too? I'll be honest with you, Penny. No, not really."

Penny nods. She's mad, I can tell. I want to make her feel better. *I think Gus is the one I'm meant to be with!* I tell her. *I think he's my person! I'm not sure of it yet, because sometimes we still don't understand each other, but sometimes we do! It's amazing! We talk to each other!*

I don't tell her that she's right about one thing: I would love, more than anything, for the people I love to understand what I'm saying. And except for Gus, occasionally, mostly no one does.

My Job

DOING MY JOB WELL IS THE best way I can reassure Penny that I'm not wasting my talents. The problem is I'm not so great at it yet. My main job is helping Gus get to know other children in the class, which I thought would be easy because so many of them (especially girls) like sitting on my mat with me. Some of them use my stomach as a pillow, which always makes me nervous. Dogs aren't great pillows because we have to breathe and scratch sometimes.

It also turns out that even though a lot of kids come over to pet me, Gus still doesn't notice them much. Sometimes he hums louder to drone out anything they might say. Because she wants to get more kids talking to Gus, Ms. Winger added to the list of rules above my mat.

Now below the two big rules:

She has added:

I know the rules because Ms. Cooper reads them to every child who comes over. She's helping me do my job, I guess. Some kids will talk a little bit to Gus. They'll ask questions like "Have you ever trimmed Chester's toenails?" or "Do you ever put clothes on him?" Both of these are terrible ideas, but still it makes me sad that Gus doesn't even seem to hear them.

I try to think of ways I can help Gus notice other kids and play with them more. I see Ms. Winger try too, but it's hard. She pairs him with Freddy, the nicest boy in the class, to play a game with, and Gus sits, twisted around in his seat the whole time to stare out the window.

There *is* one boy Gus notices, though I wish he wouldn't. His name is Ed and he isn't very nice. He still thinks it's unfair that Gus gets to have a dog in school. Sometimes he stops by our corner to say so. "I'd love to bring my dog, that's for sure, but I can't. Some people don't have to follow the rules, I guess."

Ed scares me on the playground. He pretends he's being nice and starts games like Trip Tag, which is like Freeze Tag except if you're frozen you're allowed to trip people running by you. It's an awful game. The teachers don't stop him because he's smart and plays it away from where they're standing. Sometimes during Trip Tag, Ed will hide inside a tunnel under the climbing structure, waiting for other kids to run by so he can jump out and scare them. It reminds me of the Spooky Walk and I hate it. I wish Gus didn't notice Ed, but unfortunately he does. Gus stands near that tunnel and waits for Ed to scare someone. I didn't understand why he liked it until I went to Fright Fest, and now I do: Ed is like the zombies in the park. *Ed scares me,* I once told Gus and he didn't answer. He only rocked faster in his chair because he likes hearing Ed's name.

Instead of Ed, I wish Gus would notice the one girl who comes over to my corner and talks to me every day. Her name is Amelia and she doesn't have any friends either.

Amelia is very smart, I think, but she cries a lot in school, which you're not supposed to do when you're in fifth grade. I don't think she can help it. She hates things like changes in the schedule, which Gus hates too, but usually he doesn't cry, he just squeaks and flaps his hands and sometimes he refuses to move. One thing that helps Amelia is burying her face in the side of my neck and pretending she's not crying. I don't know if she fools other people or not. She doesn't fool me because I can feel her tears.

Amelia is a math whiz, which means she goes next door to Ms. Palmer's room for an extra period every day to do advanced math work. Ms. Palmer once came in our room to return Amelia's math sheets and I heard her say, "This is eighth-grade-level math, Amelia. I'm very proud of you."

I don't think Amelia cares about math that much, even though she's good at it. She cares about the girls who won't let her sit with them at lunch. She also cares about the boys who make fun of her because she cries too much even though she can't help it.

Today Amelia feels so sad she asks Ms. Winger if she can skip math and sit in the corner with Gus and me.

"I suppose that's okay for one day," Ms. Winger says. "Remember, if Gus has to go anywhere, though, Chester goes with him."

Amelia lays her head on my side. "I wish you were *my* dog," she whispers.

I look over at Gus and notice something interesting: He's looking at Amelia. He wants to tell her something but his mouth doesn't work, so he does something I've only ever seen him do with Mama. The corners of his mouth go up. He's smiling at Amelia.

I've never seen him do this before with another child.

I look back at Amelia, but she doesn't see it. I lick her hand again and point my nose at Gus. *Look,* I try to say. *He likes you, I think. He doesn't care if you cry too much.*

Right then we're interrupted by Ms. Palmer's voice. "Amelia, you're ten minutes late for math. That means you'll be staying in for ten minutes of your recess."

Ms. Winger comes over to whisper, "Oh, I'm sorry, Pauline, I should have sent someone down to tell you—Amelia's having a hard afternoon. I told her it was okay to stay here for a little while and have some dog time."

"Dog time? Is that what you just said, Marianne? *Dog time?*"

"It helps her regroup so the whole day isn't wasted for her. If you want to give me her work, I'll be sure and have her do it later."

"Dog time isn't on the schedule, Marianne. You know that, right? Do you remember our schedule? Do you remember we're getting these kids ready for middle school? Last time I checked, there's no dog time in middle school." Ms. Palmer is very old. She wears shoes that look like they hurt her feet.

If she wasn't so mean, I'd feel sorry for Ms. Palmer.

"No, of course there isn't, Pauline. But I believe in offering students whatever support I can in order for them to have the most productive day possible. Some kids need a little more flexibility than others, right?"

Now Ms. Palmer leans closer to poor Ms. Winger, who is trying to hold her ground. "He shouldn't be here at all, Marianne. A dog in school doesn't help children get any work done. He's a distraction. That's all."

After she leaves, I look over at Gus. He's not smiling anymore. He's chewing on his hand, like maybe he is worried for Amelia. It's hard to tell for sure. Maybe he just doesn't like teachers fighting near him, but then he looks down at Amelia. He rocks a little, looks away, and then back.

He's doing something else I've never seen him do before.

He's not looking at her, but he's holding out one of his hands like he wants to touch her hand that's resting on my side. I watch it move slowly for a long time. It reminds me of the first night I met Gus—when Marc stood for a long time, almost touching his shoulder.

This feels like that. Gus never touches her hand, but he wants to, I can tell.

Which is definitely different.

Spider Watches

IT'S BEEN A HARD WEEK FOR Gus, and Sara's worried. I don't know if it's related, but ever since Ms. Palmer yelled at Ms. Winger about Amelia, Gus has been chewing on his hand more, and twice, he's wet his pants at school. It's hard to figure Gus out. He'll have a breakthrough one day when he smiles at someone like she might be a friend, and the next he'll cry for no reason and say "nis" to anything anyone offers him. That's what happened the day after he almost touched Amelia's hand. By the end of the day, Gus had cried so much Ms. Winger knelt down next to his chair and whispered, "I'm sorry this has been such a hard day for you, Gus. Would it help if you spent the last ten minutes with your sparkly pen?"

He didn't say anything, of course, but still she pulled it

out from behind her back and handed it to him, which was nice of her. Usually he has to work much harder to earn time with his pen. "We'll try for a better day tomorrow," she said, and then the next day he had one! He even laughed at a joke Ed made that I wish he hadn't, but still it was nice to see him laugh.

Sara thinks he's worried about losing me again, the way I got lost at Fright Fest. I wish I could tell her, *I don't think that's it. Something else is going on.* I wish I could tell her what I see at school: These new things seem bad, but they might also be good. I wish I could describe the way he looked at Amelia. Like he wanted to cheer her up.

Gus is getting used to me, but still, it's hard for him to have me around too much. Sometimes he likes it. Early in the morning he'll wake up and I'll hear him say hi to me. Sometimes he'll even reach out a hand for me to lick or I'll put my chin on the edge of his bed and breathe on his neck. In different ways, he tells me he likes the feel of my whiskers, but he doesn't want anyone else to know that, so those are private times. We don't let anyone else see.

Other times, like after a long day at school, he just wants to be alone, rocking in his bed and hitting his head against the wall. I get nervous when he's like that: I want to sit in his room and keep an eye on him.

"NIS!" he'll scream, and Sara will come up and take me out of the room.

I don't like to leave his room because if Gus is my person and helping him is my job, I need to stay nearby. But I also understand that sometimes having a job means lying outside someone's door and waiting for them to need you again, so that's what I do.

Some nights he lets me sleep in his room with him. Those are nice nights. If he can't fall asleep, he tells me the things that scare him. They aren't things other people are scared of, which I understand. I remember the thunderstorm that didn't scare any other dogs, only me. Gus tells me he's scared of bouncing balls at recess, of food on his plate touching, and of spiders crawling over his face at night. Out of all those things, he's most scared of the spiders on his face.

It's okay, I tell him. *I'll stay awake. I'll keep away spiders.*

I do, too, for most of the night. Until I realize that in the dark, I can't really see one and spiders have no smell, so I let my eyes close for a little while after that. But I'm here. If anything wakes him up, I'm right here.

Because this is what you do when you're a dog and you've found your person.

Principal McGregor

AT SCHOOL ON MONDAY, PRINCIPAL MCGREGOR peeks out of his office as we walk by. He's Scottish, which means everyone loves the way he talks, including Gus. He asks Sara if he might have a wee word with her before we walk to class.

"Sure!" she says, smiling. "Can Gus and Chester come too?"

She knows how much Gus loves his accent. It always makes him rock in his chair and squeak a little, which is Gus's way of saying he loves something. Usually it's fun to watch, except this time it isn't fun to hear what he says. "I hate to bring this up, but some of the teachers have been talking about Chester. One of them, specifically, is asking to see his official certification as a service dog."

"He's not a service dog, Mr. McGregor. You remember we talked about this? He's a therapy dog."

"Yes, that's right. But it turns out the state has some rules about allowing therapy dogs into a public school classroom. They need to have certification papers as well. I assume you have those at home, it would just be a matter of bringing them in so we can make copies and keep them here."

Sara looks at me and then away. She's not sure where to put her eyes. I wish I could tell her, *There's only one teacher who cares about this. It's Ms. Palmer.*

"Why are you asking about this now? Has Chester done anything wrong?"

"Oh no, the kids all love him. I love seeing him on the playground, and we can all see that he's very good with Gus. Some people are concerned, though, about the distraction factor. They say he's affecting other students' ability to concentrate. They've drawn my attention to the state regulations and apparently those are stricter than I realized."

Sara nods. I think she's trying to figure out how to tell him, *He doesn't have any paperwork. He never graduated from his program.*

"We feel like we're just starting to see some changes in Gus and we keep thinking maybe it's Chester who's bringing him out into the world more."

Principal McGregor squints his eyes at Sara. "Does Chester not have any certification papers?"

She can't lie. She wants to, though, I can tell. "He almost does. He came close to graduating, but he overreacted to loud noises during his testing. That was the only problem. He could do everything else perfectly."

"So he's not an officially certified service or therapy dog?"

She looks down and shakes her head. "No."

"But when you proposed this, you called him a therapy dog. I assumed the vest he wore meant he'd passed those tests."

She shakes her head and lifts the flap of my inside-out vest to show him. He reads the truth: "SERVICE DOG IN TRAINING."

"Oh dear," he says, shaking his head.

"Technically the state doesn't legally mandate those papers to work as a service dog. You just have to demonstrate to a judge that the dog assists in necessary activities of daily living that the disabled person is unable to perform for themselves."

Mr. McGregor shuffles some more papers. "But Gus has an aide for those things. Chester doesn't do any of that."

"No, I know. But Chester's helping Gus in a different way. You know how hard we've been trying to avoid an out-of-district placement. We want to find a way to keep him here, in this school and home with us. I believe Chester is doing something we haven't been able to do, even with everything we've tried. He's helping him *connect* with other students. He might even be helping him communicate with them."

"If he's not certified, we can't have Chester in school. I don't have any choice in the matter."

"Maybe if I petitioned the school board?"

"It's not their jurisdiction, I'm afraid."

Sara nods and looks down. "I understand. Can he go to class today so the other children can say goodbye and Gus can have one day to adjust to this? It would help him, I think."

"Yes, I suppose that's all right. A transition day for everyone."

Sara stands up to go just as Gus makes a low growling sound. Up until this point, I didn't know if he understood what Mr. McGregor said. Now I know. He understands more than most people think.

"Come on, Gus, let's go," Sara says. "We'll talk about this in the hall, okay?"

He doesn't move.

"Gus? Can you hear me?"

I nudge the hand on Gus's knee. *It'll be okay,* I tell him. *We still have today and I'll be at home waiting for you after this.*

Gus keeps growling.

I'm not sure he can hear me. *Let's show him how you've changed. Let's stand up and walk out of here.*

"Gus?" Sara says. "Should I count to three?"

I don't understand how Sara can know Gus so well and not know how much he hates when she counts to three. His friend Mama knows this but his real mama doesn't.

"You know it just occurs to me we're meant to have a fire drill today," Mr. McGregor says. "You say the dog hates loud noises—will he be okay with that?"

He's already forgetting my name and calling me "the dog."

"Of course *Chester* will," Sara says, because she's noticed the name thing too. "He'll be fine."

She's dropped her nice, polite voice. She's so mad she takes Gus's hand without counting to three and pulls him up out of his chair. "Come on, sweetheart, we're going to class now."

How to Say Goodbye

ALL DAY I WORRY ABOUT THE fire drill. I don't know if fire drills are the same thing as fire alarms. I can't tell Gus I'm nervous because it'll only make him more nervous. We haven't looked at each other since we left Mr. McGregor's office, but I know he understood everything because all morning he keeps one hand on my back, which he's never done before.

He's never needed to, I guess. Now he does.

It means I don't lie down at all. I sit beside him, awake, so he can keep that one hand on me. Just before lunchtime, when Ms. Winger says she has a bit of sad news to share with the class, I put my chin on Gus's knee because I think she's going to tell us about the fire drill, but no.

"We're going to have to say goodbye to Chester today. He'll come back to school to visit occasionally, but he's not going to come to school every day and stay in our room anymore. It turns out there are some rules about having dogs in school that Mr. McGregor didn't know about when he said it was okay."

Amelia lets out a terrible, strangled-sounding cry. She runs over from her chair across the room and flops down next to me. "IT'S NOT FAIR!" she screams.

Ms. Winger keeps her voice calm. "We have to abide by those rules even if we don't think they're fair. Amelia, I have to ask you to wait until the end of the day to say goodbye to Chester. I'm telling you now because I want you to have a chance to think about this and get ready for it. Remember, there's a way to say a nice goodbye so you don't scare Chester or any of the other kids. You think about how to do that, okay? Let's go to lunch now, everybody. Single file and quiet. Amelia, come up here and talk to me if you need to, but let Gus take Chester to the cafeteria."

Amelia can hardly peel herself off me.

It's surprising, though. This whole time, Gus has kept one hand on the same place on my back. Which means that Amelia has touched and hugged his hand. She's probably kissed it too, judging by the number of kisses she's given me.

But he hasn't pulled away.

Maybe he's worrying about me as much as I'm worrying about him.

I don't know because we're both too nervous to talk to each other.

My Person

MS. WINGER KEEPS HER PROMISE. AT the end of math period, she tells the kids they have twenty minutes to do free reading. "If you want to spend a few minutes with Chester to say goodbye, you can," she adds.

Amelia knocks over her chair she stands up so fast. A few other kids come over too.

"One at a time, please. Amelia, why don't you wait until the end?"

Most of the girls come over and hug me. One of them clips a barrette to my collar so I'll have something to remember her by, then two others do it too. Now I have more barrettes than I want poking me in the neck, but that's okay, I think. Especially after one of them whispers in my ear, "Don't worry. We'll all be nice to Gus when you're not here," which makes me feel better.

When the girls are done I can tell a few boys want to say goodbye, but they're a little shy. It's hard to show how you feel sometimes. I understand that. The soccer boys line up and each one pats me quickly on the head. "You were a great ball fetcher," one of them says.

"We'll miss you, Chester," another whispers.

They make no promises about being nice to Gus. They've never been nice to him, but they've also never been mean. They just pretend he's not there.

One person who makes me mad is Ed, who sees everyone else saying goodbye, so he gets in line too. When it's his turn, he asks to shake my paw, then he turns around and tells the two boys behind him, "I'm the one who taught him how to do that."

No, he isn't. Even the other boys seem confused, like they don't believe him.

"I *did*," he says. "It was early on, right when he first got here. He'd never learned shake because dogs for crazy people don't need that trick, so I taught him."

He says "crazy people" softly so only the other boys hear him. They nod and laugh a little. Ed isn't funny but they're all scared of him.

When it's finally Amelia's turn to say goodbye, I'm surprised. She isn't crying. Instead, she hugs my neck and says, "You're the best dog in the whole world, and I'm going to miss you so much! I want to tell you something—"

Just as she lifts up my ear to whisper into it, a terrible shriek pierces the room.

My heart races. I drop to the ground. I have to get under something. Amelia holds on but I claw myself free and crawl toward the coats.

The shrieking sound pulses and won't stop. The coats are a bad idea. They fall off their hooks and won't help me. I want to hide under something but Ms. Winger is saying everyone needs to go into the hall.

I can't go into the hall. The hall has no desks and nowhere else to hide. I race back to the room and get under a desk. I don't think about Gus. I can't think about him with all this noise.

Then I remember: It's the fire alarm.

It's loud and it's terrible but it won't last forever.

The noise is still going, but I crawl out from under the desk. I look for Gus right away. I feel terrible that I left him. I panicked, but now I'm not panicking anymore. Other kids are in the hall, lining up quietly.

"Single file, everyone!" Ms. Winger calls. "Single file outside!"

I don't see Gus anywhere. It makes it hard to breathe. There isn't any real fire, but the noise feels like a fire in my head.

Gus isn't lining up with the other children. Ms. Winger doesn't see this, but I do. Amelia screams, "Come on, Chester! Come out with me!"

NO! I bark. *I can't leave Gus.*

The kids start filing out. Ms. Winger doesn't understand me. She doesn't see that Gus is missing. Maybe she thinks he ran outside when the alarm started? I lift my head and smell. It's hard for my nose to work with all these kids and the noise pressing down. I can't tell if he's still in the hall.

Finally Ms. Winger comes over and touches my head. "Come on, Chester. I don't see him. Gus is probably outside. We'll do our count there—don't worry, we'll find him."

Ms. Cooper, who is supposed to be watching out for Gus, is dealing with some other kids. I don't think he's outside, but I can't be sure. I smell something, but it's far away. It's telling me not to go outside. "Come on, Chester," Ms. Winger says. "You need to come now."

I definitely smell something. It's him. It's Gus. I know it.

"I'm getting your leash, Chester. I can't leave you inside by yourself."

The noise has stopped, which helps me concentrate. Ms. Winger clips the leash onto my collar, which is okay, I think, because now I can lead her to where Gus is. He's not outside, he's in here, up the hallway, and he's in trouble.

Sometimes I can smell trouble before it comes. Like Amelia before she has a meltdown. My nose wakes me up so I can do what I can, which usually isn't much. A dog nuzzling a knee doesn't stop a meltdown, but sometimes it helps.

This time, though, it's worse.

It's not just a meltdown.

"Come, Chester," Ms. Winger says, pulling me toward the door to the playground. "Right now. We have to get outside to the other children."

I sit down so she knows: *NO. I won't go that way.* I pull her the other direction.

"Chester—"

I pull harder so she knows: *I mean it. This way,* and she follows. I've got my nose to the ground where the smell is strongest. There are chemicals in the smell, and other things I don't recognize. It's Gus, too, though, and it's getting stronger. I know this is right.

I get to a door and Gus's smell is all around me. I scratch and bark because there's a doorknob and my paws won't work for opening the door. We have to do it fast. He's in trouble, I know.

Ms. Winger opens the door and screams. She's surprised but I'm not, because Gus is my person and a dog always knows when his person is in trouble. Gus is on the floor of the janitor's closet. He's wet his pants but that's not the worst part. The worst part is that he's asleep and even when I lick him and lick him and lick him, he won't wake up.

Never Run Away Again

I DON'T UNDERSTAND. I LICK GUS'S HAND because I know he doesn't want me to lick his face. When he still doesn't wake up, I get so scared, I lick his face.

Nothing.

Ms. Winger doesn't understand either. She calls for help on her cell phone and has to answer questions for the person on the other end. "I don't think he drank anything in here. I don't see any evidence of that . . . He's unconscious, but he's breathing . . ."

"The ambulance is coming, Chester," she says when she's done talking on her phone. "You did a great job, didn't you? You knew he wasn't outside. Can you wait here for a minute with him while I get some help?"

She doesn't leave for long, but while we're alone I talk to Gus. *I'm so sorry I ran away. I won't ever do it again, I promise. We'll practice every day and I'll never run away again.*

I don't know if he can hear me.

If he can, he doesn't say anything.

Pretty soon, Ms. Winger is back with Mr. McGregor. "Oh, poor boy," he says first, then into the black box he usually wears on his belt: "Have we got someone outside to tell the paramedics where we are?"

Ms. Winger holds Gus's hand while we wait, which he ordinarily doesn't like, but I think it's okay now because he's asleep.

"You should know that Chester is the one who found him," she tells Mr. McGregor. "I thought Gus was already outside. Chester forced me to come this way and look in this closet. If he hadn't been here it would have taken another twenty minutes to find him. Maybe longer."

There's a sound up the hallway. Mr. McGregor steps out of the closet. "BACK HERE!" he calls to two men who wear uniforms and are pushing a rolling bed.

After that, there's a lot of commotion. Two men lift Gus up and strap him to a bed that has wheels on the bottom so they can roll him outside. I follow them out to a big white car. After they've got him inside it, one of the men looks at me. "Does this dog belong to him?"

I can tell Mr. McGregor isn't sure what to say. "Yes, he's not an official service dog, but he works for this boy, yes. He found him just now."

"We can't bring a service dog with us unless there's someone at the other end to take charge of him."

"Right, of course. Then he'll stay here with us."

A few seconds later, the truck door is closed and another loud pulsing noise stabs my ears. I do everything I can not to run away. I tell my legs that Gus needs me to stand right here. I tell my legs, *Look what happened just now when you got scared and ran away.*

"You're a good dog," Mr. McGregor says. He's nice enough to bend down and pet my head while the noise moves away from us. "His parents will be at the hospital to take care of him. Don't you worry. He'll be okay."

That makes me feel better.

"Why don't you come inside and stay with me? I'm sorry about all this, laddie, but we'll get you sorted out."

I'm not sure who Laddie is or why he's calling me that.

By the time Marc picks me up from Mr. McGregor's office, I feel like I've been there for hours and my nerves are raw from the sound of the telephone ringing all the time. Mostly

I haven't listened to his conversations, but I did listen when I heard him ask the other person how Gus Stevenson was doing.

"Very good, okay. Thank you so much, then."

His door opened and a secretary leaned in. "What did the hospital say?"

"Yes, they've confirmed it was a seizure and they've admitted him for some monitoring. He'd never been diagnosed with epilepsy in the past, but they think he's had three or four seizures in the last few months."

I wonder if "seizures" is another word for having accidents.

"His father will be here in an hour to pick up the dog."

"Is this really Chester's last day?" the secretary asks.

"I'm afraid so. It seems a shame, especially after what he did today, but I haven't got a choice really."

She shakes her head. "Such a sweet dog. We'll all miss him, won't we?"

"Except for Pauline, I'd say yes."

"That's right. Except for Pauline."

How to Worry More

GUS DOESN'T COME HOME AT ALL that night.

Sara comes home late, in the middle of the night. She turns on the kitchen light quickly where I'm sleeping and turns it off again. "Sorry, Chester. Don't wake up."

That's all she says.

I don't know where Gus is or if he's going to be okay.

Earlier Marc came home to give me my dinner and take me for a walk. While he was home, he made a few calls and told whoever he was talking to that they didn't know too much of the story. Presumably Gus ran into the custodian's closet to get away from the fire drill and something in there—one of the chemicals in the cleaning agents maybe—triggered what he called a grand mal seizure. "They have to keep him in the hospital for observation. Right now, they've got him hooked up to machines to see if he has another . . . You can imagine how much he hates that. The poor guy had to be sedated before they could attach the electrodes to his head."

The only thing I know about hospitals is that Penny's father died in one. It had something to do with his heart. She went to the hospital one afternoon and I didn't see her for a whole day. When she finally came home, she was very sad.

All night I have trouble sleeping.

I exhaust myself so much I don't even wake up the next morning when Marc and Sara leave. Instead of our usual morning routine where they eat oatmeal and make jokes, they're gone when I get up and my food bowl has my breakfast in it.

It's a terrible feeling—eating food you haven't watched them fix. I don't even feel like eating, except after a few hours, I do.

Later Cora, a neighbor who is scared of dogs, stops by to let me out. She thinks she needs to keep me on my leash even though we're standing in our fenced-in yard. I feel so silly, I have a hard time peeing.

Eventually, I do. Instead of saying, "Good dog," or telling me how my family is doing, she says, "Finally," and brings me back inside.

Home Again

MARC AND SARA DON'T COME HOME again until just before dinner. I'm so happy at the sound of the car in the driveway, I run around downstairs carrying one of Gus's shoes in my mouth.

"Oh, silly dog, put that down," Sara says. She's in a good mood, I can tell, because she bends down to hug me. "He's home, Chess! They let him come home!"

I notice she doesn't say he's okay.

Maybe that doesn't mean anything, though.

I also notice he doesn't eat dinner with them that night. "He's so tired," Sara keeps saying. "The doctor says it'll go away once he's used to this new medication. It's just hard to watch him sleep all the time."

From their dinner conversation, I learn a few things. Apparently, Gus has been having seizures for a while. So far, they've been little ones that make him zone out and sometimes wet his pants. He's probably had headaches that he hasn't been able to tell anyone about, and maybe other issues—blurred vision, confusion. They think the fire alarm made him panic and triggered a bigger seizure. This is as much as I understand. They talk about medicines and side effects and a special diet. It sounds like they're saying, "No cardboard at all, or very little anyway."

I don't understand until Marc says it again, sadly: "Oh, poor Gus. He loves his carbohydrates."

Sara talks some more, mostly saying there's a lot they don't know and they'll have to wait and see.

"So that's it?" Marc says. "They send us home with two prescriptions and we wait and see if it happens again?"

"The hospital says he has to stay under observation by a nurse trained in seizure protocol for the next two weeks. It's possible he's been having seizures every time he's had an accident."

Sara looks sad. She's not eating her food. "Which means he has to go back to school with a nurse who will stay with him the whole time, watching for a seizure. I hate the idea of him having one more adult around him. Do you think the other kids see him as the strange boy who hardly talks and is surrounded by adults all the time?"

Marc pats her hand. "Yes, Sare, I do. Not to us or his teachers. But to other kids who don't understand what he means with his squeals and his flapping—yeah, he's the strange kid in the corner surrounded by adults."

Now Sara is really sad. "Why does everything just keep getting worse? Having autism isn't hard enough, I guess, we have to have seizures on top of it too."

Marc comes over and puts his arms around her again. "One fight at a time," he whispers into her ear. "We take all of this one fight at a time."

My Bed

IN THE MORNING, I FEEL SO nervous about Gus going back to school with a nurse at his side that I scoot out behind him and almost make it into the car, before Marc holds his foot in front of the door. "Sorry, Chester, remember the new rule? No dogs at school."

I want to tell him: *Gus doesn't need a nurse at school. He needs me.*

Sara gives me a hug. "I'm so sorry, Chess, but remember? Mr. McGregor said you can't go to school with Gus anymore." She stands up. "Oh, look at him, Marc, he *wants* to go. He *knows* what's going on."

Of course I do, I think. *She knows I do.*

All day at home with Sara is like being with Penny the day

after I failed my test. Sara tries to work, but she's distracted and thinking about other things. Her computer's on but she keeps coming into the kitchen, where I'm lying on my bed. On her third trip in, she lies down on my bed with me. "I wish you could be there with him," she says. "I just keep worrying that he's sad and alone . . ."

I want to tell her that Gus isn't as sad at school as she thinks he is. I remember what she said before school started—that she wanted him to find something that he loved. I wish I could tell her, *He loves Mama. He loves the dish room. He might even love Amelia or at least like her a little. But Mama is the main one.*

I don't think anyone knows this except me. They think he likes watching the steam come out of her machine, which he does, but what he really likes is Mama. He likes the way she puts one finger between the plates as she loads them into the machine so they don't make a sound. He likes how she pulls the glass racks out at the other end. He likes how she says, "Hello, my boy. How you doing today?" It makes him laugh inside. He doesn't laugh on the outside because it confuses him to hear himself laugh. He doesn't like that sound, so he laughs inside.

I wish I could tell Sara, *He's not alone. He'll visit Mama today.* She'll probably tell him it's good to see him again. She might not know about the hospital. She might say, "Where you been hiding, my boy?" And he'll rock and laugh inside at that.

I wish I could tell Sara, *It's not so sad,* but I can't. Or I do, but she doesn't hear me.

For a while, it's nice lying together on my bed instead of hers. Then it gets a little uncomfortable and she says we need to wash my cover, it doesn't smell good. That's where she's wrong. It smells great to me—full of memories and good times when I've found dead animals to roll in. I hope she doesn't wash it, but she doesn't hear that wish either because that afternoon, I come back to my bed and my cover is gone.

How to Not Talk

THIS SCARES ME: IT'S BEEN MORE than a week since his seizure, and Gus still hasn't talked to me once. I've been trying every evening, asking different questions like: *How was the hospital? Did you see any dead things? I like seeing dead things, but maybe that's not true for people.* Now I ask: *How's Mama and her steamy machine?*

He doesn't answer. Maybe he's mad at me because I can't come to school anymore.

I want to come to school! I tell him in the morning while he's getting ready. *I wish I could! Mr. McGregor said no!*

For a long time, he eats his oatmeal and doesn't say anything. *Do you want me to come back?* I finally say. He might say no, I remind myself. He might say, *I don't like the way the girls crowd around me to pet you. You cause too much commotion.*

I can't blame him if he says this, because it's true. He doesn't know I'm there for him, doing a job. He doesn't know that I found him in the closet. It's not his job to remember everything I do for him or say thank you.

He doesn't answer my questions. *That's okay,* I tell myself. *Gus is still my person, and I still have a job, I'm just not sure what it is these days.*

I want to remind Sara about teaching me to read. Even if it doesn't work for me, it might help Gus get more interested in using a word board or his computer. He has those things, he just never uses them. Sara's forgotten about that idea because now she has another idea that's taking all her time.

She's reading the laws about service dogs. It turns out there are some exceptions to the rules with children who have autism. "Apparently, if we got a judge to approve of Chester as a service dog because of Gus's autism, he'd be allowed to go into the public areas of school with him, like the cafeteria and the playground. The classroom isn't considered a public area, so he'd have to stay in the main office for most of the day, but Gus could take him outside for recess and when he goes to lunch. Is that a terrible idea?"

Mark makes a face. "That sounds like a dog spending a lot of time in an office where a dog isn't really meant to be."

"But he'd be *there*. Gus could visit him any time he asked to."

Marc bends down in front of her. "Can you picture Gus asking to visit Chester in the principal's office?"

She puts her hands over her face and shakes her head. I think she's saying no, she can't picture it.

I can't either. Gus doesn't ask for me out loud. But there're a lot of things he likes and doesn't ask for out loud. Like Mama and her dish room. Like sparkly pens. I remember Penny once saying, "Part of your job will be understanding what your person needs even if they don't say it." I think that she was right, but how can I do my job if I only see Gus a few hours in the afternoon when he's too tired to talk?

That night I go into Gus's room like I always do while he's getting ready for bed. I watch Sara brush his teeth and hold his pajama bottoms open.

I don't think he'll say anything because I've sat here every night since he's come home from the hospital and he hasn't said a thing. Still, I want to be here if he does. I think about some of our old conversations. When he told me the things he's afraid of. When he said he loved his parents but sometimes they touch him too much and it hurts his skin. I remember this and never get up on Gus's bed the way I get on the bed with Sara.

Tonight, instead of waiting for Gus to say something, I start talking to myself. I can't help it. I tell him I've been lonely sitting at home with no one but Sara, who has her own job to do. *I wish I had a job again,* I say. *And someplace to go like school.*

I don't mean to sound pathetic. I'm afraid I do anyway, but now that I've started I can't stop. *It's quiet at home. I liked being at school watching out for you. I liked going out for recess and all the smells of science time and stopping by Mama and her machine.* I sound like someone who hasn't had anyone to talk to in months.

Gus climbs into bed without looking at me.

Sara comes in first to kiss him good night. Marc comes in later to sit with Gus for a bit and pat his back in the right rhythm. Marc likes to hum as he does this. I don't think Gus likes the humming, but I do. It makes me sleepy enough to curl up on the rug next to his bed.

Even though I've spent all day sleeping, I'm tired from all the talking I just did. I'm tired because it's hard being around Sara's worry all day. Even when she's working, she's thinking about Gus. She's wondering if she should call the school to check on him. She's staring at me like she'd just feel better if I could go back to school again.

Even if you're pretending to sleep through all this, it's tiring.

Great Family Pet

AFTER TWO WEEKS WITHOUT A SEIZURE, everyone agrees that Gus isn't in any immediate danger anymore. Sara tells Marc the nurse doesn't need to stay with him in the classroom any longer, which makes her feel a little bit better, but not much.

Everything is back to the way it was before, except Gus takes pills now and sleeps more and I don't go to school with him.

"Chester is a great family pet," Marc says, trying to cheer Sara up. "And he's here every afternoon for Gus to come home to."

I don't know why "great family pet" seems like a sad, disappointing thing to be. I guess when you know how good you feel doing a job, you want more. You just do.

Maybe I want too much.

At night when I run outside for my last pee, I don't even bark anymore to the other dogs nearby. I feel like I don't have anything to say to them.

Sara knows how I feel. She feels it too.

One day at lunch, she looks up from her soup and says, "I know, Chess. I know you don't want to be home here with me."

I look at her carefully. I wasn't saying anything just now, but I wonder if she's heard me other times. I do an experiment that afternoon. I sit outside her open office door and say, *There are raccoons right now, digging through the garbage.*

There aren't really, but I know she hates raccoons and the mess they always make. If she can hear me, she'll jump up and start banging pots and pans.

I wait. For a second, she turns her head from the computer as if she hears a bird, maybe. Or something else in the distance. And then: nothing.

No, I decide. She doesn't hear me.

A Mystery

TODAY THERE'S A NEW MYSTERY.

I know a little bit about mysteries from the TV shows I used to watch with Penny. She liked the ones that featured people who weren't typical detectives because they were blind, or had something I never understood called OCD. She liked them because usually the person's weakness made them a good detective. Like the blind guy could smell some clues better than other people. (Most people are such poor smellers, it doesn't surprise me that a decent one can get his own TV show.) Watching those shows has taught me enough to know right away that I'm looking at a possible crime when Gus gets off the van from school and there's a big bandage across his nose. There are also two dark circles under his eyes. He looks like he's wearing a mask or very bad eye makeup.

Sara screams when she sees it, then puts her hand over her mouth. "Oh my God, what happened, Gus?"

He doesn't say, of course. He gets around Sara by walking the same way he does at school—up on his toes, pressed close to the wall.

Sara opens his backpack and pulls out the blue book where there is a note from the nurse that she reads aloud: "Gus had an accident on the playground late in the day today. He was on the far side of the climbing structure where teachers couldn't see him. When they called, he came out from under the structure with a cut on his nose. He was taken to the nurse and cleaned up, but he couldn't tell us how he'd gotten the cut. We left a voice-mail message. The nurse thinks that his injury might look worse than it actually is."

Sara is mad and I don't blame her. I'm mad too.

"He's autistic!" Sara screams, even though Marc's not home to hear her, only me. "Of course he can't tell her what happened!"

Gus has only been home for a little while but already his face looks worse. The purple circles under his eyes are getting bigger and blacker. Sara puts ice on his nose, which he doesn't like. He moans and says "nis" and makes it worse by touching his nose and crying when it hurts.

"I'm taking him to the hospital. I think he might have broken his nose. Don't you think I should take him to the hospital, Chester?"

I don't like hospitals because I don't know what happens in them but I do agree it looks bad. Gus lies down on his bed and I can see blood crusted inside his nose—I want to lick it but I stop myself.

When Marc gets home, Sara tells him what Mr. McGregor said when she called the school. "There was a substitute nurse, which is why I got that strange note that didn't take any of his seizure history into account. Apparently there was another child under the wooden climbing structure. He didn't know Gus was under there until he heard him crying, he says."

It was probably Ed, I say. *Ed isn't nice and whatever story he told is probably a lie.*

Of course she doesn't hear.

I go over to Gus, who's curled up on the sofa. *Did Ed do something to you under the climbing structure?*

He rolls over so I can't look at his face.

I put my chin on his leg. I don't really need him to answer.

I know it was. Before I left school Ed started playing a new trick on younger kids where he offered to push them on the tire swing and then wouldn't stop or let them off when they started to scream. Gus probably stood too near the tire swing and got hit. That's my guess. I wish Gus could tell them this himself. If he can't, I wish they could understand me so I could tell them.

Sara thinks it's something else. "He obviously had a seizure, Marc. We need to get him to the hospital and have him checked."

Sara is pulling on her coat, but Marc doesn't move. "Not everything is a seizure, Sare. You remember they told us that."

I take a good sniff around on Gus's leg. I remember the way he smelled when I found him in the closet—sharp and metallic. He doesn't smell like a seizure now.

"He was by himself underneath the play structure. He's a seizure-prone child and they let him wander away to a dark tunnel where he couldn't be seen. I don't understand what they were *thinking*."

"They were letting him play with another kid. That's what we've always *wanted*."

"Not anymore. He could have hurt himself. He *did* hurt

himself. *Look at him, Marc.*"

"I have, Sara. I think the nurse is right—it might look worse than it is."

"If it looks bad, it *is* bad. He's obviously had a seizure on their watch and they don't want to admit it because it means they'll have to hire the expensive nurse again. It's infuriating!"

"Look, I agree there's a problem, but we don't have to assume the worst right away. I'd like to talk to the teachers and wait a little bit to see what Gus can tell us."

"*See what Gus can tell us?* Do you hear yourself? Gus can't tell us anything! That's why we have to protect him! Being nice to the school doesn't help him!"

"If we storm over to the school this afternoon, what are we going to ask them to do? Keep Gus inside every day at recess? They'll just tell us it's time to consider the out-of-district placement and send him so far away we'll only see him on the weekends."

This conversation is so sad I move to Gus's head and sniff at the back of his ear. *It's not your fault they're fighting,* I whisper. *This is what grown-ups do.*

Gus rolls over and looks at me. His face looks even worse than it did a little while ago. For the first time in days, he looks me in the eyes. It's hard to look back in his. They're purple and yellow now.

But still, I can see something in his face. He's trying to tell me he didn't have a seizure.

Ed did this to him.

I don't want Gus to be sent away. If he's sent away, I really won't be able to do my job. I need to find a way for Gus to tell them what happened.

How to Tell On Someone

AS SARA READIES A BAG TO take Gus to the hospital where he doesn't want to go, I try to distract her with other things.

"No, Chester, not now," she says. "Look at this, Marc, Chester thinks it's time for a walk because I've got my jacket on. I'm sorry, Chester—no walks now. We have to go. Cora will stop by later and take you for a walk."

Oh, if only I could tell her that Cora never leaves the yard for our "walks." They're not really walks, they're embarrassing trips down our back steps and back up again.

"Do you need to go pee, Chess? Marc, can you let him outside before we go?"

Marc opens the door but I don't move. I need them to stop

what they're doing and think for a minute. Gus didn't have a seizure. Gus had boys on the playground do something mean to him.

I didn't understand why Gus liked to stand near the tunnel where Ed hides. It was dark and loud and scary to me, so I didn't stay. But Gus is different from me. He's afraid of many things, but he likes dark, scary places. He likes Fright Fest and Ed, and that spot underneath the climbing structure is like visiting Fright Fest every day. Ed plays mean games there. He jumps out at little kids. That's his idea of recess fun.

Gus is crying now. He doesn't want to go back to the hospital.

Tell them, I say. *Tell them what happened.*

Marc says, "Are you going to call ahead or just take him to the ER and wait?"

"I'll call, I guess. Does that mean you're not coming with us?"

"I'm not sure it helps to have us both there. Plus, someone should walk Chess. He's obviously antsy. Why don't I come in a few hours and give you a break?"

No! I say, sitting again near the chair. *Talk to Gus first!*

"Come on, Gus. I've got your bag packed. It'll be okay. I've got your headphones and your music and two sparkly pens. You can't have them both at once but we'll play games while we wait. Come on, babe, let's go."

He's sitting up now. He's dressed with his shoes on and a jacket over his shoulders. He doesn't want to go, I know, but it's more than that. His feet are glued to the ground.

He can't go. He can't move.

Can you tell them what happened? I say. *Did Ed do this to you?*

For the first time since he's gotten home, I hear him speak. He winces. *Yes.*

It's harder to hear his inside voice now because his outside voice is getting louder. His mouth is saying, "Ba . . . ba . . . ba . . ." because his ears don't want to hear what he's saying. His mouth can't tell his mom and dad what happened, any more than mine can.

It's okay, I say. *Go with your mom. We'll figure out a way to tell them what happened.*

He doesn't stand up right away, but eventually he follows his mom out to the car.

After they leave, Marc paces around for a long time. I follow him into his bedroom because I'm nervous too and I don't want to be alone. I watch him change his clothes.

I watch him lie down on the bed, read a newspaper for a minute, then stand back up. I watch him walk into the bathroom, pull a string through his teeth, and walk back out. Finally, he takes me for a short walk and then says, "I'm sorry, Chester, I've got to go check on them. I've got to find out what's happening."

He fills my bowl with food two hours before dinner and sloshes some water next to it. "You'll be okay, right? Do you want me to leave the radio on?"

We're all nervous, remembering the last trip to the hospital. *No radio,* I say with my eyes. I need time to think and make plans.

"Yeah," he says. "You're right. The radio is dumb."

Dark Night

I HEAR MY DOG FRIENDS IN THE distance, barking at the moon, and the sound makes me feel lonely and sad. I don't have anything in common with these other dogs. A language maybe, but what does that mean when we see each other on the street and have nothing to say? My heart is with my people.

When they finally get home, Gus is with them, which is a relief, but they're all tired, I can tell. They turn on the light by the front door and whisper to each other. "I'll get his medicine," Sara says. "You take him up to bed."

After all this waiting, that's all I hear. No one says anything to me.

The next morning, Gus stays home from school. The

bandage over his nose is bigger now and he looks like he's wearing sunglasses underneath except it's his skin. Purple-yellow skin-sunglasses.

After breakfast, Sara calls the school. "Mr. McGregor, please," she says in an unfriendly voice.

It makes me nervous.

I get up from my bed and sit near the phone so maybe I can hear what he says on the other end. Sara sees me and says, "No treats now, Chester, you haven't even eaten your breakfast yet."

I do like my treats, but this isn't where I sit to get them. How can I make her *understand*?

When she starts talking to Mr. McGregor, she moves around so much I have a hard time following her conversation. "The hospital couldn't determine if he had a seizure or not, but this incident has shaken our faith in the school's ability to keep Gus safe. Marc and I have talked about this and we both agree that we can't send Gus back to school . . . For the time being, we're going to keep him at home . . ." She opens the refrigerator and closes it again. She moves over to the table and sits down. "He wasn't safe at school, Mr. McGregor. The doctors have already written letters in support of this idea. If you want to stop by our house and look at Gus's face, I'm sure you'd agree with me as well."

Poor Sara, I think. Gus can't tell her what happened. She has to do *something,* and this is the only thing she can think of. I hear other snippets. She calls her mother and tells her the whole story. "The hospital's answer is to increase his medications until he does nothing but sleep all day . . . I don't know what else to do . . ."

Her mother must ask about me—because she leans over and pets my ears. "No, Chester's not allowed at school anymore because he's not an official service dog. I talked to the principal again about this, and he said the most they could allow would be for Chester to come to school during recess time. He isn't allowed back in the building. I don't see much point when he gets swarmed by the little girls on the playground. I don't think Gus goes near him outside."

I move closer to Sara so she knows I'm listening to all this.

It isn't true what she's saying. Girls swarm me for a few minutes on the playground and then they leave me alone. The rest of the time, I spend with Gus. *If I went back I could at least watch out for Ed. I could keep Gus away from him. That would be something.*

"No, he was never trained for that . . . Yes, he was the one who found Gus . . . right . . . I've read a little about that . . .

Maybe I'll do some research . . . It's not a bad idea . . ."

After she hangs up, instead of telling me what she was talking about on the phone, Sara spends the rest of the day taking care of Gus and researching on the computer.

"Do you want to hear what I learned today?" she tells Marc the minute he walks in the door that night. "Remember we talked about making Chester a seizure dog, but we assumed that if he didn't pass the standard service dog training there's no way he could learn something this specialized? Well, guess what?"

Marc smiles. "He can?"

"Not yet. But he *might* be able to. Here's what I found out. There are seizure response dogs who are trained to recognize when a seizure is happening. They get help, fetch medicine, move their person away from stairs, things like that. Dogs can be trained for that part using trainers who know how to mimic seizures."

Marc looks down at me. He hasn't seen me mail a letter or open a door. He doesn't think I can do these things.

"But here's the most interesting part. About thirty percent of the dogs who work with epileptic people develop the ability to alert them fifteen to twenty minutes *before* a seizure begins. They can *sense* it before the person feels *anything.* Isn't that amazing? No one has any idea how they do it."

Smell, I tell her. *We smell it.*

"They think it might be smell but they've done all these tests and their machines don't detect anything."

I remember the afternoon of Gus's seizure at school—how I finally found him in the closet. It was a scary smell. It made my heart race.

"It also could be they notice finger twitches or changes in breathing patterns."

No, I say. *How would I notice that?*

"They say maybe it comes from having a connection to the person. Some dogs tune in to their person, but wouldn't be able to recognize a seizure in someone unfamiliar."

Sure, I think. *Seizures smell terrible, but so do lots of people for different reasons.*

"Because it's so mysterious, there's no way to train the dog to do it. They can't practice the skill by finding people on the brink of having a seizure, so the only way for a dog to get qualified is by doing it once. That's all it takes!"

"And if a dog proves he can do that?"

"Then we could tell the school it's medically necessary for him to be in the classroom with Gus!"

Sara's so happy at this prospect it makes me nervous. I go to the TV room, where Gus is watching a TV show by himself, which I've never seen him do before. Usually he watches TV only when his parents force him to watch something with them. I didn't think he knew how to turn it on. I didn't think he was interested. I sit down next to him and watch for a little while. It's a show about people who get dirty for a job. I don't understand it. *Are you really watching this or are you having a seizure?*

I'm watching.

And the point is they get dirty doing this stuff?

It's funny.

We watch for a while. A man gets covered in black soot and smiles at the camera. Behind him, there's steam coming from a machine. It looks a little like Mama's machine.

Does your face still hurt?

A little.

Do you want to go back to school tomorrow?

He doesn't answer me. After a long time, I realize I probably shouldn't have asked. It ended our nicest conversation in a while.

Funny Sounds

───────── ❧ ─────────

I STILL THINK GUS SHOULD GO BACK to school, but I have to admit it's nice having him around all day. He doesn't mind if I sit near him while he watches TV. If I don't ask too many questions, he'll sometimes answer one or two. I have to ask the right ones, though. If I ask a complicated question like *How do these two people know each other?* he won't know. If I say, *What's that sound?* he'll laugh and rock and say, *A clicking! It's funny!*

Gus loves funny noises so much that if he doesn't hear one for a while he'll make some himself. Funny noises make me nervous, but now I'm getting used to the ones Gus makes. They don't scare me anymore. I don't love them, but that's okay.

Gus loves them, and I love Gus.

★ ★ ★

One night I follow Gus into his room and he surprises me.

What are you doing? he says.

It's bedtime, I say. *You're putting on your pajamas.*

But why are you here?

For a second I'm not sure what to say. *I always come in while
you get ready for bed.*

You do?

Yes. Has he really never noticed?

Do I need you here?

Technically, no. Just making sure.

Okay.

He hadn't noticed, I guess, but that's okay, I tell myself.
He's noticed now.

Martha Speaks

I KEEP BEING SURPRISED.

Every morning I expect Sara to send Gus back to school and every morning she says, "Not today. I don't think he's ready."

Gus doesn't mind. He's happy to wear his pajamas over to the sofa and spend the day there. He's found a new show called *Martha Speaks.* It's about a dog who eats something called alphabet soup and the next day starts talking.

That's like you, he says.

Except not really, I say. *She's yellow and I don't really talk.*

You don't? He's confused, I can tell.

Not out loud. I'm more like you. I talk other ways.

Isn't this talking? he says.

I'm not sure how to explain the difference. *Our mouths don't work well. We think-talk. Most people don't understand us. In fact no one does. It's not a great way to communicate.*

I don't know if Gus hears me. He always stops listening if I talk too long.

The problem is, Sara's getting sad and frustrated, I can tell.

After researching for a while, she's decided she can't send me back to school as Gus's seizure alert dog. "It's too hard to prove," she tells Marc. "You need witnesses who see the dog react *before* the seizure happens. We've never seen that. He reacted beautifully during the fire alarm at school, but that was *after* the seizure. I don't know if it's worth the fight. The longer I keep Gus at home, the more I wonder if he was getting anything out of being there."

I think Sara is happy to see Gus watching TV because it's different and seems more normal than staring out the window. At first, I liked it too because watching TV together reminds me of happy times with Penny. Now I'm surprised that Sara thinks it's okay.

Watching a lot of TV means long periods of empty time where neither one of us says anything.

I keep reminding Gus about the nest we watched the birds

build. There are baby birds in it now that he hasn't seen. He either doesn't hear me when I mention it or doesn't care, because he never looks. I do, though. The baby birds are big enough now that I can see their little beaks peeking up over the edge of their nest. They're waiting for their mother to bring them food. It's quite a sight.

One morning I ask if he thinks about Amelia at all. *Do you wonder how Amelia's doing without us there?*

Who? he says, staring at the TV.

This isn't good, I think.

What about Mama? I say. *Don't you want to go back to school and see her again?*

I can tell he's listening because he almost turns and looks at me.

Maybe she'd let you press one of those buttons.

He rocks back and forth at this idea. I know he wants to.

You'd have to go back to school first.

No school, he says.

You can't stay home watching TV all day. It's not good for you. I'm surprised to hear myself say this, but I keep thinking about Penny. Too much TV watching wasn't good for her either.

Yes, I can, he says.

Watching so much TV makes him sound a little bit more like a regular kid. The minute I think this, though, he goes back to watching TV and doesn't say anything more.

Two days go by.

Then three.

It's hard to remember what yesterday and tomorrow mean—they all look the same. One morning after breakfast, I hear Sara on the telephone. "Yes, thank you, Mr. McGregor. Marc and I have come to a decision. We're not going to send Gus back to school, and we're not interested in sending him away to a residential program. Instead, we're going to ask that we go ahead with the homeschool program we talked about. We'd like a certified ABA teacher here from nine in the morning until noon. In the afternoon, I'll need paraprofessionals here working on activities of daily living. I've got two doctors' letters and I've also hired a lawyer to negotiate all this with the school."

I know about lawyers from the TV shows I used to watch with Penny, how they show up only when everyone is unhappy and can't get along.

After she hangs up, Sara stares at the phone for a while.

"There," she says. "I did it."

Eleanor

A FEW DAYS LATER, A TEACHER NAMED Eleanor comes to the house. Sara talks to her for a while in her office. I sit outside the door but I can't hear what they say. When they come out, Sara turns off the TV and sits down next to Gus on the sofa. She tells him things are going to be a little different from now on. "You're not going back to school anymore, Gus. I hope this is okay with you. We just weren't sure if you were learning anything there or finding things you liked to do."

She waits to see if there's any reaction from Gus. There isn't.

Tell her about Amelia! I scream. *Tell her about Mama!*

He doesn't.

"We've talked to Mr. McGregor and he agrees that all children still need to learn even if they don't go to school, so he's sending some nice teachers to come here and teach you at home."

Maybe it'll be Ms. Winger! I want to sound hopeful, like maybe this idea isn't all bad.

"Today a teacher named Eleanor is here, and she's waiting in my office. That's where you're going to work with her. From now on, there won't be any TV in the morning. You'll have to do everything she says and then you can earn some TV time in the afternoon."

My heart starts to race. This doesn't sound good. It's hard to picture Gus sitting with a stranger in Sara's office. There's a window in there but it's not our window. He doesn't like being alone with teachers who ask him to do things he doesn't care about.

I don't stay with Gus for the first session, so I don't know how it goes.

Gus doesn't speak to me afterward but goes straight for the TV that Sara has promised.

For the rest of the afternoon, he watches one show after another after another. He doesn't say or think anything that I can hear when I ask him how it went.

How to Sit

AFTER A FEW DAYS, THE TEACHERS let me come into Sara's office while they work with Gus. It isn't always Eleanor, the first teacher who seems the strictest. There are others who bring tote bags full of flash cards and toys that are meant to catch Gus's interest, except they've got all the wrong toys. They've brought cars and music boxes and Mr. Potato Head dolls. Gus doesn't like any of those things. Gus takes one look, sees there are no sparkly pens, and doesn't care anymore what's in their bags.

These women are no-nonsense. They have commands they give Gus and responses they expect from him. They've set up a low table with a bumpy cushion like Gus used to sit on at school, but here he's not allowed to squirm around like he used to do at school. Now they say, "Gus, come sit," and pat the bumpy cushion on the chair beside them. When he doesn't move, they don't get mad, they just go over to the window where he's standing, take one of his arms, and steer him to the table. "Gus, come sit," they say, and give him another chance to do it by himself. Then they push him down.

"Good sitting," they say.

After he sits, they pull out a stack of flash cards with pictures on them. "Gus, point to cat," they say. He's got three choices: a fire truck, a cat, and a ball.

He points to the cat.

"Good pointing to cat, Gus."

More cards. More pointing.

"Point to chair, Gus . . . Point to notebook . . . Point to belt . . ." I'm amazed at how many cards they have and how many times they reach down and pull more out of the bag. I keep thinking this will be over soon and we'll move on to something else. But it isn't and we don't. All morning long, Gus sits in his chair pointing at all the pictures of words both of us know but can't say out loud.

It reminds me a little bit of working on flash cards with Penny, and how I was going to learn to read, which I've never done.

In the evening I hear Sara explain this to Marc. "According to them, the whole problem with nonverbal kids is no one really knows what their receptive vocabulary is. They need to know what he's capable of before they can focus on getting him to talk."

"But we know Gus is smart. Have you told them how much he understands?"

"Yes, of course. They say they need to do the tests for themselves." I can tell Sara is starting to wonder about all this. "Supposedly this is a pretty successful program. I keep thinking we should stay with this for a while and see what happens. Then I stand outside the door and listen to what they're doing and it seems so repetitious. Like it's never going to get him talking, it's just going to drive him crazy."

Marc stares down at the floor. "He talks, Sara."

"No, he doesn't, Marc. Not *really*. He can repeat what we tell him to say and phrases he's heard on TV, but has he ever told us something that happened to him during the day? Has he ever told us what he's *thinking*?"

Marc shakes his head.

If only I could tell them everything he's said to me.

One teacher who comes to the house is a little different from the others. I think she knows Gus is too smart for this, because she asks him questions that are a little harder. She lays out pictures of three different dogs and asks, "Hey, Gus, can you point to the dog who *isn't* black and white?"

That time Gus makes a joke and points to me. If I could laugh, I would. It's the first joke he's made in weeks and it's nice to hear.

This teacher's name is Lindsay and she laughs too. "You're right! Chester isn't black and white, is he? How about the dogs in these pictures? Can you find one here?"

He can of course.

I think it makes him sad doing these dumb things. It makes him miss Mama and the way she wasn't afraid to show him how her complicated machine worked because she knew he could understand complicated things, even if he can't talk about them. Sometimes the hours with these teachers go on so long Gus can't stand it anymore and pushes all the cards off the table. Once, he turned the whole table over.

I'm surprised that the teachers don't get upset at this. They stay very calm and say, "You'll have to clean this up, Gus." When he doesn't do it, they take his hand and make his hand clean up every card. When they're done, they say, "Good job cleaning up, Gus." With these teachers, getting mad isn't a good way to tell them anything.

At the end of the week, they show Sara their tally sheets and tell her that Gus has a receptive vocabulary of over a thousand words. "That's excellent," they say. "Really excellent."

I remember Penny talking about my vocabulary to prove how smart I was. *What good does a big vocabulary do,* I think that night, curling up on the floor beside Gus's bed. Gus hasn't talked to me at all since these teachers started coming.

We have all these words and neither one of us can think of anything to say.

An Idea

I'VE GOT AN IDEA!

If Gus can tell his parents that Ed was the main problem at school, they'll know it's okay to send him back as long as someone keeps him away from Ed's scary tunnel on the playground.

If he can just say "Ed," that would be enough, I think.

They'd call Ms. Winger and ask about Ed. She would know. Even if she didn't see what Ed did to Gus, she would know that Ed was the problem. She heard him complain about Gus getting special treatment. She knows that if Ed had a chance to be mean to Gus without anyone else seeing, he would take it.

This is the hard part, though: How can I get Gus to say "Ed"?

I get my idea while we're watching TV at the end of the day.

After all this time watching, I've decided my favorite shows are the commercials. They're often about food and they're easy to follow. There's one commercial that's on a lot with a man named Crazy Eddie who sells cars for rock-bottom prices. At the end, he spells his name in shaving cream on car windows. "Just remember," he says while he spells. "E-D-D-I-E is crazy. Crazy Eddie."

Even though Sara and I haven't worked on Penny's flash cards and I can only pretend to read, I know that letters spell words and "Ed" sounds like the first two letters of "Eddie." I have watched Crazy Eddie spell those letters many times. Though I don't have fingers and I can't use a shaving cream can, maybe I can do something else.

At dinnertime that night, I try using kibble bits dropped on the floor beside my bowl. It's messy and doesn't work. I move one kibble with my nose and all the others move with it. When I stand back, it doesn't look like two letters, it looks like an old blind dog who can't eat properly has been here.

While everyone else is asleep, I get another idea. I pull a few items out of the trash and lay them out in what looks— to me at least—like two clear letters: *ED*.

All night I feel excited about the message I've written. I imagine Gus coming downstairs, reading this, and saying, "Ed," before his brain has a chance to get confused and stop him. I picture Sara understanding at once and calling the school.

Except it doesn't happen this way.

Instead of Gus reading my note first and understanding what it says, Sara comes down, sees the crumpled napkins and watermelon rinds, and screams, "BAD DOG! NO GARBAGE!"

Marc cleans it up before Gus even sees it.

Now I feel worse than I've felt in weeks. Sara thinks I'm no better than an untrained puppy, burrowing in the trash can for food scraps.

That night I don't even go upstairs and watch while Sara helps Gus get ready for bed. Ordinarily I think of this as part of my job. I listen to what Sara says and to Gus's noises. I learn a lot about their day by hearing all this. But not tonight.

Tonight I lie downstairs on my bed and wonder if I'll ever be able to help Gus.

It Does Get Worse

THE NEXT MORNING OVER BREAKFAST, SARA tells Marc she's going to call the school today about having more curriculum sent over for the teachers to work on. "I'm not sure how much more Gus can take of these drills and this testing. If we include more substantive material at home, I think his behavior will get better, don't you?"

Yes, I think. *It will.* But it isn't the answer. The answer is for Gus to go back to school.

"Maybe," Marc says.

"If they could at least read some *books* with him. Or do some history. This was going to be the year he finally got to learn the American history that he loves. Now he's missing it all."

Marc shrugs. "We don't know that he loves it."

"Yes we *do*," Sara snaps. "We *do* know that he loves history. He *loved* going to Williamsburg and seeing all those people dressed in old-fashioned costumes. Why do you think he loves Fright Fest so much? He thinks those are real people from olden times who've come back to tell him stories."

Does he? I wonder. I feel as if I know him so well, but of course I don't know everything. His mother knows him better.

Eleanor is the teacher today, the strictest one, and also the one who doesn't think Gus understands very much. Today she starts by laying out three flash cards. "Okay, Gus, can you point to the blue ball, please?" I feel my eyelids getting heavy. Recently these sessions have gotten so boring, I've started sleeping through most of them. Eleanor doesn't seem bored, though. She thinks her tests have gotten trickier, which I guess makes it interesting to her.

"Gus, can you put the blue block *in front* of the orange block and *beside* the yellow block?"

He does it. She smiles and writes a note on her forms.

After a while, I wake up to this: "Gus, can you make one

tower of six blocks and another tower of *fewer* blocks?"

I don't know what "fewer" means, but Gus does.

"Good job, Gus!" she says, clapping her hands.

This time when I fall asleep, I wake up to screaming. Gus has pushed all the blocks and even Eleanor's notebook off the table. Eleanor doesn't seem upset, even though Gus is yelling right next to her. When he stops to take a breath, she says, "I see you're upset, Gus. After you're finished being upset, you'll have to clean this up."

I smell Sara standing outside the door. She's trying not to make any noise, but she's standing there, I know.

"Are you ready to clean this up, Gus?" Eleanor asks.

More screaming. It's terrible to watch.

Gus's face is red and his nose is dripping. I want to stop the crying. I also want to lick the drips away. Eleanor doesn't care about either of those things. She pushes me away, says, "No, dog!" and stands up. "I'm going to step out of the room and talk to your mom. When you're ready to clean this up, I'll come back and help."

Gus stopped crying when she pushed me away. I think he notices things like this and maybe he even worries about me, though it's hard to tell because he doesn't say anything. In the quiet, I can hear their conversation in the hall. "He's doing so well, Sara. This behavior is to be expected because he's really making strides. I see this all the time. With any kind of progress, we're going to hit some resistance. We've had a very productive session. *Very* productive."

I can't hear what Sara is saying, so I go over to Gus. *You don't have to do this, you know.*

He doesn't say anything.

If you go back to school you could stop these boring lessons and see Mama again.

Too much talking doesn't work with Gus so I choose my words carefully. I keep talking because he's not screaming anymore. I think that means he's listening.

You were happier when you went to school. Maybe you didn't love everything about it, but you liked enough things and you got through the other parts.

I can't tell what's happening. His face is still red from crying. He's rocking in his chair. I move a little closer but I'm careful. I don't go too close or try to touch him.

His breathing is still loud.

I don't know if he's heard what I've said.

I try this: *Do you want to go back to school?*

He holds his breath for a long time like he's thinking about it.

Maybe.

It's very soft, but I hear it. His voice. I'm so happy I can't stop myself. I put my nose on his knee and lick his hand. He pulls it away. *I'm sorry,* I say. *I know you don't like that.*

"YOU DON'T LIKE THAT!"

His voice sounds louder and different this time. His mouth moved when he said it. He wasn't talking through our minds. He really talked.

You just said that! I say.

Maybe I shouldn't get too excited. He repeated what I said, which we've heard him do before. Still, this feels different. He didn't repeat a nonsense word or something he heard on TV. If he repeated one thing I said, maybe he can repeat something else! Maybe I can say what he needs to tell Sara and he can repeat it!

I have I an idea. I can help you tell your mom what happened with Ed.

"You don't like that," he repeats.

Why not? It's a great idea! I'll go slow.

"You don't like that."

Okay, you don't like that idea, but why not?

"You don't like that."

That's when I realize: He's not hearing me at all. He's

listening to the sound of his own voice. How it fills the room and comes back into his ears.

"YOU DON'T LIKE THAT!" he yells again. Now he's smiling.

The door opens. Sara and Eleanor are right there.

"What don't you like, Gus? Can you tell us what you don't like?"

He's laughing and rocking in his chair, so Sara laughs a little. "What's happening here?" Eleanor asks Sara. To her it must look crazy—a few minutes ago, he was screaming and pushing everything off the table. Now he's laughing and rocking back and forth.

"I don't know," Sara says, because of course she doesn't.

No one looks at me. No one thinks maybe the dog got Gus to say a full sentence.

Tell her about Ed! I shout from behind Sara. *Tell her: Ed hurt me in the tunnel under the playground structure. It was only Ed, so it's okay, I can go back to school. They just have to make sure Ed doesn't come near me.*

He doesn't say any of it. He makes his old squealy sounds instead. *Tell her: Ed hurt me! That's all! Just say that!*

I wait. Sara waits.

Say it.

Sara doesn't mind waiting. She's been waiting his whole life to hear what he's thinking.

Now. Ed hurt me.

"Eh—Eh—Eh!" he says into his hand, then he flaps his hand around like it's got the word and it's trying to get rid of it. But it's not Ed's name.

It's not even close.

It sounds the same as all of Gus's noises that don't mean anything.

Sara tells him it's okay and gives him a hug. "I think you need a break, sweetheart. Eleanor, can Gus have a break and then come back and help you clean up?"

"I suppose," she says, though I can tell she's not supposed to give him a break before he cleans up. There are lots of rules to her kind of teaching.

"I'd like to have a minute to talk to Gus in private, if that's okay," Sara says.

"All right," Eleanor says, then stops at the door. "Maybe the dog should come with me, too? Just so there aren't any distractions?"

No! I'm not a distraction!

"No, he's fine," Sara says. "He can stay."

Now Eleanor is mad and clicks the door shut very loud

behind her. It's like everyone is saying things without using any words now.

Sara kneels in front of Gus again. "This is it, babe. I need you to look at me and tell me: Do you hate having teachers at home? Do you want to go back to school?"

I can hardly believe it—she's asking the right question! I hold my breath and wait. I don't say anything because I don't want to confuse Gus. I'm worried that when I talk, he assumes everyone can hear me.

Silence.

Finally I can't stand it. *School!* I whisper. *Gus, say, "I want to go to school!"*

Gus's eyes go to the window.

"Can you help us, Gus? Dad and I want to know what you think. Were you ever happy at school?"

Yes. Tell her yes, you had friends! You were happy sometimes!

"Can you make a choice—school or home? You just have to say one word. Maybe if I put out flash cards and you pointed?"

His whole face goes to the window. It's not even his window. He doesn't care what's out there, he just wants to escape from this room and her question and all this pressure.

"You don't like it . . . ," he whispers for the umpteenth

time. He's got one sentence his brain is saying today and he wants to use it for every question he's asked.

"Gus, please—if I find the cards, can you point to one?" She's touching his arm and looking through the flash cards spread all over the floor. If he doesn't say anything, she'll assume he wants to stay home. Home is easier. It might be more boring with teachers who don't teach him anything, but home has TV, and if he can't watch TV, it has his window where he can lose himself for hours.

SAY SOMETHING TO HER! I scream, but he doesn't look at me.

That's when I smell it.

At first I think something has spilled, like a bottle of chemicals. It's sharp and metallic. I think maybe it's going to blow up like the lighter fluid Penny once used on a grill that scared me. I bark to get everyone out of the room. First at Sara, then I go over to Gus where the smell is even stronger. It's coming from the window or from something outside, I think. *Get away from the window!* I try to push him with my head and that's when I realize, it's not the window. It's Gus.

Gus smells like chemicals.

Like he's going to blow up.

I bark for Sara to help.

"What is it, Chess? What's wrong?" I keep barking. *"Calm down,"* she says.

Eleanor comes back in. "All right, I have to tell you—this is why I can't have the dog in here during lessons. We'll lose ground every time he goes off like this."

I hardly hear what they're saying because I have to focus on Gus. With all my energy I have to get him to hear me: *Sit down,* I say. *Get away from the window.*

He's starting to wobble. He's swaying toward the glass pane.

MOVE! I scream and then I bark like crazy.

Sara's up just in time. As Gus starts to fall toward the pane of glass, she grabs him. He's having another seizure and this time we can all see what it looks like—the shaking, the twitching, and the white bubbles in the corners of his mouth.

Even though it's hard to watch, there's no sound at all, which means my heart stays calm and I do the only thing I can think of. I stretch out beside him with my face near his and I wait for it to be over.

How to Say Yes, Part Two

GUS DOESN'T SPEND THE NIGHT IN the hospital the way he did after his last seizure. This time Sara and Marc bring him home before the sky gets dark. Gus looks okay, but he's moving slower, like his legs hurt or maybe his head. Something must hurt, because he's walking right next to Sara and letting her put her arm around his shoulder.

"Right over here, sweetheart," she says. "Let's get you to the sofa."

He bumps into her and then bumps into the sofa, which is not like him.

I'm scared that maybe seizures make people not act like themselves.

Sara sits him down and kisses the top of his head. "We'll

get you up to bed in a minute but first I'm going to get you some water. Are you okay here?"

Gus nods. "Okay," he says.

Now I'm really scared. He just answered her question, which means he's *really* not acting like himself.

Sara stops walking and turns back to look at him. "You're okay?" she repeats.

He doesn't look up. "Okay," he says again, and smiles. She looks at Marc. Even though he's repeating what she just said, this feels different. She's asking him a question and he's answering her. It feels very different.

She brings him his water and kneels in front of him. "Are you ready for bed? The doctor said this medicine will make you feel sleepy."

"Feel sleepy," he says. His eyes flutter a little like he's already half asleep. I'm almost sure we're all thinking the same thing: It's like he's so tired his brain can't operate in its usual confusing way. It can't stop him from talking. I can tell Sara wants to keep him up a little longer and find out more.

"Can we ask you this question again, babe?"

Gus's head bobs a little, almost like he's nodding.

"Do you want to stop having teachers come to the house? Would you rather go back to school?"

Marc steps up behind her and touches her shoulder.

"Don't, Sara. He's too tired for this. Let's put him to bed and talk about this in the morning."

She turns to Marc and snaps, "No. This is our *chance*." She goes closer to Gus and kneels on the floor in front of him. "Gus, can you stay awake a little longer?"

His eyes open again. He looks right at his mom and smiles. She smiles back. I've never seen him do this before. It's nice.

"Can you tell us if you want to go back to school?"

Tell her yes, I say. I know he can hear me, because he looks around the room to see where I am and where this voice is coming from. When he finally sees me, he smiles and nods.

Tell her yes! Tell her the only problem at school was Ed!

He nods again.

"Gus?" Sara says. "Can you tell us whether you want to go back to school—yes or no?"

"Sara—" Marc is behind her.

"He can do this, Marc," she snaps again. "I see it in his eyes. He knows what I'm asking. He wants to tell me."

I move closer. I don't say anything. I wonder if he's not answering because he thinks his mother can hear me. Maybe he thinks the answer is already out there, that she already knows about Ed because I've said it so often.

For Gus to speak, I have to be quiet and not say anything at all.

He opens his mouth. "Chester—" he says.

Sara's hand goes up to her mouth. It's the first time she's heard him say my name. It's not a repeat of something she's said. It's his own thought coming out of his mouth.

"Wants . . . school."

Sara gasps and hugs Marc because she doesn't want to scare Gus by hugging him right now. Then she kneels in front of him. "And do *you* want that too? Do you want to go to school with Chester?"

He nods first so we know his answer. "Yes," he says softly. "See Mama."

Now Sara's crying and can't stop herself from hugging him. "I'm right here, sweetheart!" She spins around to Marc. "Did you hear that?" she says. She sounds breathless.

Marc is right behind her, hugging them both. They're all so happy. "Your mama's right here," Sara's saying, really crying now. "I'm right here."

I don't think it matters that he's thinking about a different Mama. I'm the only one who knows the Mama he loves at school, but it doesn't matter.

We've finally done it. We've told them enough.

We've told them what they needed to know.

How to Make a Plan

ALL MORNING LONG, SARA'S ON THE phone. As far as I can tell, the plan is to send Gus back to school, but only if I can stay with him all day as a seizure alert dog. "Yes, Chester can predict Gus's seizures," Sara tells Mr. McGregor on the phone. "We had his teacher here as a witness, so it won't be hard to prove." So far, she's talked to a doctor and another specialist. She's making lists and nodding as people on the other end of the phone tell her what she needs to do.

It's been a few days since his seizure and Gus hasn't been talkative like he was the night he came home from the hospital, but it's okay. He knows the teachers won't be coming to the house anymore. He knows we'll be going back to school soon. He and I haven't talked privately about any of this, but I think if it's a choice—if Gus only has the patience to talk silently to me or out loud to his parents—it's better for him to talk to his parents. They need to hear what he has to say. They can do more to help him.

Since I've come to live with Gus, his biggest change was talking to his parents about school, but there have been other changes too. Some are so small they're hard to notice. Like looking at Amelia and trying to smile. Like visiting Mama every day. He needs to do more of these things so that other people actually see them.

He will, I think.

I'll be there to help him and he will.

We just have to wait for the school to get organized. Sara keeps talking about "getting protocols in place and paperwork cleared up." While she's busy making arrangements, Gus and I are free to watch TV, which is nice. In the middle of one of our favorite *Martha Speaks* episodes, I hear the doorbell, which hasn't rung once since the teachers stopped coming to the house. It worries me that maybe they've changed their minds and decided to come back.

But no. I go to the front door and there is Penny talking to Sara. Even though it's confusing to see her here again, it's impossible for me not to say hello. I jump around and lick her hand and bring her a shoe to say hi.

"Oh, sweet dog, I'm happy to see you too!" Penny says, bending down and hugging my neck. "So, so happy."

Even though Penny just got here, it sounds like she and Sara are in the middle of a conversation. Like maybe they were talking on the phone earlier and I didn't realize it. "How long do you think you'd need to teach him all this?" Sara asks her.

"It's hard to say. Chester's always been such a fast learner, but what do you want him to be doing exactly?"

Sara pulls out a notebook. She's made a list like she always does. She starts reading: "In the event of a seizure, Chester will need to move Gus away from stairs and windows. He should stay nearby to help him sit down or lie down. He should press the emergency alert button Gus will be wearing around his neck. After that, if Gus is safe and the seizure is over, he should leave Gus and get help from an adult. He should go first to the teacher, then to the nurse."

I look at Penny. *I can learn all this quickly! You remember how smart I am!*

"Maybe a month?" Penny says.

Sara frowns. "Would it really take that long? We want Gus back in school as soon as possible, but we don't want him there without Chester. The school has agreed if he masters seizure-response skills with a certified trainer. I know this is a lot to ask, but we were hoping it might take a week, or maybe two at the outside."

Penny thinks about this for a moment. "The only way I could do that is if I brought Chester home with me and worked with him there. Training like this needs to be done intensively, about eight hours a day."

Sara looks confused. "Doesn't he need to be with Gus for this?"

"No, it's better if he isn't actually. The point is to generalize Chester's responses to as many different situations as possible. The person won't change, but the places will."

Suddenly I feel worried. Penny's talking too fast. She looks nervous the way she looked in front of the group at the farm.

"I guess you know best, but I'd think you'd want to do that kind of practice with Gus."

Yes, I tell Penny. *I should do it with Gus.*

She pats her skirt. "To be honest, it's such hard, repetitious work, I'd hate to put Gus through that. I'd rather take Chester home with me, do the hard part myself, and bring him back, all trained and ready as a seizure-response dog."

"I don't know. Gus has gotten very attached to him. Wouldn't you be willing to come to the house and work with him here so he can still spend his evenings with us?"

Penny closes her eyes as if she's giving this idea some thought. "It's not a good idea. These are challenging skills and they won't be easy to learn. As smart as Chester is, I'd like to have his attention as focused on me as possible."

"Oh gosh—" Sara smiles down at me and picks up one of my ears to rub. "We'll miss you so much, Chess. I hate to let you go for even a week."

I look up at her. *It's not a good idea,* I say with my eyes. *Something bad might happen to Gus if I leave for a week.*

Sara smiles at me. Sometimes I think she almost hears me and then ignores it because if she heard a dog talking, she'd be crazy. "Aren't we being silly—look at Chester's face. It's like we both want to cry." She bends down and whispers in my ear, "It'll be okay, sweetheart. When we get you back, you and Gus can go to school together again."

When she stands up, she's all business again: "Okay, I'll pack up his things. Move, Chess. I want you to have your bed at Penny's house."

I move off my bed. She piles my bowls, puts some food in a bag.

"I'd like Gus to come down and say goodbye before you go—"

"I don't have a lot of time," Penny says. Instead of seeming less nervous, she seems more nervous now. She's looking at the door, pressing her hand to her head.

"This won't take long, I promise."

Sara goes into the TV room to get Gus.

Even though we're alone in the room, Penny still won't look at me. In her heart she must know that this isn't a good idea. I go close and nudge her hand. *It's me,* I try to say. *If you watch me with this family, you'll see—this is where I belong.*

She pets me a little, but won't look in my eyes.

Sara walks back in with Gus beside her. "Okay, Gus. Chester's going away with his old friend Penny for a little while. We're all going to miss him, so we have to say goodbye before he goes. Can you say 'Goodbye, Chester'?"

Tell her no! I say to Gus. *Tell her Chester doesn't want to go.*

He hears me. I see it in the way his expression changes. His whole face turns.

Say no! I repeat it slowly: *Tell her Chester doesn't want to go.*

His body starts to rock. He goes up on his toes. I inhale but don't smell a seizure coming. This is my chance.

He opens his mouth. "Nis," he says softly. So softly, even Sara doesn't hear.

Louder! I say.

"Time for us to get going," Penny says. Gus makes her more nervous, I can tell. I think Penny's afraid that maybe she's like Gus in some ways.

Penny clips on my leash—Gus doesn't say anything. She moves us toward the door.

"Wait!" Sara says.

I turn around and go back to Sara as far as the leash will let me. "Don't you need his vest? You can't practice in public places without it, right?"

"Oh yes," Penny says. "Thank you. That was silly of me."

Sara pulls it off the hook in the mudroom where it usually hangs.

A minute later, we're gone. Penny jogs me out to the car and opens the front passenger side where I always used to ride. I thought I missed it, but now I'm not so sure.

I don't want to leave Gus.

I don't want to wonder what's happening back here and have no way to know.

In the car, Penny starts talking the minute we've pulled out of the driveway. "She didn't mention your reading program once! Not once! You're lived there for—what, four months?—and this whole entire time, the only thing she's thought about is herself and her family. Gus this, Gus that, the whole time I was there. Oh, it makes me so angry! Is she trying to say she didn't have time to work with you for twenty minutes a day on your reading? That was all I asked for. What a waste."

It's not a waste to think about Gus. That's my job. She's been helping me do my job.

"I'll tell you something, Chess. The first thing we're going to do when we get home is work on the flash cards and test your vocabulary. I want to see how much you've regressed living with those people."

I don't know what "regressed" means. It's not a word in my vocabulary. *No,* I try to tell her. *We promised to work on seizure-response skills. I only have a week to learn them, remember?*

She doesn't answer me, of course. Even if she could hear me I don't think she would. She's not good at back-and-forth conversations like this.

Penny's House

PENNY'S HOUSE LOOKS THE SAME, BUT feels different.

It's sadder this time. And lonelier.

The TV is too loud. Even Penny's voice seems louder. Right after we walk in the door, she throws my vest in the corner and pulls out the old word flash cards. Even though I haven't worked on them this whole time, I try to remember what they say so we can move on and she can teach me the jobs I'll need to know.

"Yes!" she says, when I get my fourth word right. "You've retained it all, you amazing dog! I can't wait to tell my new friends! I've joined an online group for people doing serious research on canine-human communication. They all agree teaching your dog to read is the most practical first step in talking to your dog."

Really? I look at her. My heart feels heavy.

"There's one woman who's posted videos of her dog reading twenty-six different commands. Some people have accused her of doing off-camera cuing, but I believe her. I look at how quickly you've learned these words and I know some dogs are just extraordinarily smart. Some people have never met a dog like that, so they're skeptics. But I'm not."

The more Penny talks about this, the more scared I feel. I wonder when she's going to teach me what I need to know about responding to seizures. She hasn't mentioned it once since we left Gus's house.

I feel hopeful for a few minutes when she says, "Now we're going to take a break from reading to do something else."

Great, I say, and start toward the closet where she put my vest.

"We're going to work on getting you to *point* to the cards I say. I'm going to lay down two cards and get you to touch one of them with your nose. Like this, see?" She touches one of the cards with her own nose.

I think about Gus with his home teachers, touching their flash cards.

He touched a lot of them and never told them anything. I wonder if I could learn to read enough words to say to Penny: *Take me back. Gus needs me.*

I don't think Penny will teach me those words because she doesn't want to hear them.

She lays out two cards. They look different on the floor. I can't tell what they say. "Chester, point to 'down,' please."

They both look like 'down.' I don't know what to do, so I lie down.

"No, Chester. Sit, please."

I sit again.

"*Point* to 'down,'" she says, and does something she's never done before. She puts her hand on the back of my head and pushes my nose toward one of the cards.

"Yes!" she says when my nose hits the card, hard enough to hurt. "You pointed to 'down'!"

She lets my head go and switches the cards. "Okay, can you point to 'down' now?"

Her eyes go from me to the card she wants me to choose. It's easy to tell which one it is. I don't want to point to it, though.

My nose hurts from what she just did. I'm not reading and I don't want to learn tricks where I pretend like I am. I don't see how that will help Gus.

"Do it by yourself, Chester. I know you can. Point to 'down.'"

I look at her, not at the cards. I tell her with my eyes: *Don't make me do this.* I want her to understand: We're both better than this. She raised me to believe that serving my person was the most important thing I could do with my life. "I'm not your person," she told me many times. "You'll know who your person is the minute you meet them—that's how it usually works." I must have looked worried, because after she said that, she reached over and hugged me. "Oh, Chester, I promise it'll happen for you. You're my smartest, best dog yet. Everyone will love you." Now I've learned: I don't need everyone to love me; I just need one person and I've found him. She doesn't understand that Gus is my person. He has been since the first time he saw me and screamed and I thought, *I can help this boy be less afraid.*

I *have* helped him, I think. He *is* less afraid. He's talking a little more. He's told his mom and dad he wants to go back to school, but he can't go if I'm not with him, and Penny isn't teaching me what I'll need to know for that.

"Point to 'down,' Chester," she says again.

I don't move. I hold my head back so she can't push it again.

"Chester. Are you listening to me?"

I do something I've never done in one of our training sessions before. I turn around. "Chester?"

I walk away. My heart is beating hard. I've never disobeyed a command in my life.

"CHESTER!" Penny gasps. "What are you *doing*?"

I think about her father's heart attack. I don't want her to have one. I look over my shoulder to see if her face is red or sweaty, two heart attack signs I learned from a commercial. Except for her expression, which is horrified, Penny's face looks fine. I keep walking.

"CHESTER, STOP!"

I don't.

I go over to the door and sit down beside my vest that lies on the floor. *If I wait here all day without moving, maybe she'll understand what I'm trying to tell her,* I think. But she doesn't.

She thinks I've lost all my training in the time I spent living with Gus and his family. "I don't understand," she keeps saying.

For the rest of the day we go outside and work on the old basic commands that I learned when I first came to her house. I guess she wants to see if I remember them. I sit. I stay. I heel.

What about the new things I need to learn? I ask her. *What about the emergency alert buttons and fetching medications? Teach me those,* I beg her. *Like you promised Sara.*

But in the two hours we work outside, I don't learn anything that will help me with Gus.

Tower Puzzles

I'VE BEEN WITH PENNY FOR TWO days now and she hasn't taught me anything about responding to a seizure. Instead, she's setting up towers and mazes made out of cardboard boxes. She says they'll help me increase the flexibility of my thinking.

"Once the neurological pathways become flexible, your brain is more capable of joint communication. Remember, Chess, look to me for help. I'll cue you on how to open the doors and get the treat. That's how you'll get to be a more interactive thinker."

I don't want to be interactive! I tell her. *I want to go home to Gus!*

This morning, she's set up a circular cardboard tower with

three doors. Each door has a string attached to it. Judging by the way she looks at the strings, I'm pretty sure I'm meant to pull one of them.

"So here's the point, Chester. Monkeys can learn that if you pull the right string, a door will flap open with your treat. Some canine experts think that dogs' weakest area is problem solving. They say you have to be taught everything by rote because you don't understand cause and effect. I don't think they're right. I think you can figure this out if you've got enough motivation. That's why I've got your favorite treat ready to go—" She pops open a Tupperware, releasing a wonderful smell I remember: beef brisket. My nose lifts. My mouth waters. I used to work long afternoons for Penny's beef brisket.

Those are happy memories. Those were the days when she still talked about the important jobs I'd do for my person. I try to imagine what she'll tell Sara when she takes me back and I can't do any of the things Sara asked me to learn.

Suddenly, a terrible thought occurs to me: *She's not worried about what she'll say to Sara because she's not planning to take me back.*

I look around the living room where Penny and I have

always spent most of our time. I have everything I need here. My bed, my food dishes. As she puts the brisket treat into the cardboard tower, I look in the pantry and my stomach does a turn: She's got two shelves of dog food cans and a full container of kibble. Why did she buy so much dog food if she expects me to stay for only a week?

My heart begins to race. Dogs might have a hard time learning cause and effect, but we don't have any trouble understanding food and what it means: Penny's planning to keep me here with her. She doesn't think working with Gus is as important as me learning to read and talk by pointing to cards.

Realizing this makes me so nervous I don't know what to do. Maybe I can sit by the door and refuse to do anything or go anywhere except back in her car. Maybe if I concentrate on these reading lessons I can learn the only words I want now: "Take. Me. Home."

Gus can't go back to school without me. I have to be there with him. Not only to press his button and move him away from stairs if he has a seizure, but to steer him away from Ed and toward other people like Mama and Amelia.

After a morning of working on flash cards and the string-draped castle, which I'll never understand, we take a break for lunch in our old favorite spot, on the sofa in front of the TV.

I used to love sitting here, finding out about people and the world outside this house by the TV shows we watched. I learned all about criminals and the detectives who catch them. I learned that it's people you don't expect who turn out to be criminals. Like Penny, who is stealing me and committing a crime and eating lunch as if everything is normal.

"Come on up on the sofa, Chester. You know that's okay." She pats the seat beside her. "Did those people not let you up on their furniture? Were they like *that*?" She rolls her eyes as if this is just another reason not to like them.

I don't get up on the sofa.

I sit nearby but I don't look at Penny.

"What's wrong, Chess? You're in such a mood this morning. Aren't you happy to be back home?"

I look at her and look away.

"I don't understand you. Remember when you didn't want to go with those people at all? When I had to force you and tell you everything would be okay?"

Wait a minute, I think. *I do remember that, but how does she?* I move closer and try to catch her eye. *Could you hear what I was thinking back then?* I ask. I wait for an answer.

Nothing.

I move to another spot, where she can see my face. *I want to learn my job for Gus,* I say. *I want to go back and be with him.*

I watch her face carefully. I don't think she hears my voice, but there's a thought in her head that she doesn't like. She looks down and shakes her head.

I move closer so my face is under hers. *You shouldn't keep Chester here. It's not right. It makes you a criminal.*

I'm trying to sound like her own brain talking to her. I'm not sure if it's working. She shakes her head again and picks up the TV remote to raise the volume.

Penny's Mom

"WE HAVE TO GO SEE MY mother this afternoon," Penny tells me the next morning. "I don't want to go any more than you do, but we don't really have a choice, I'm afraid."

This is interesting, I think. We've been to visit her mother a few times before. She's very old and lives in a nursing home where they take care of people who have problems remembering important things, like their daughter's name. Whenever we go, Penny has to start the visit by saying, "I'm Penny, your youngest, remember?" Sometimes she has to remind her again while we're there. "I'm not Olivia, Mom. I'm Penny. Olivia is my sister and she lives in Florida now."

I always like visiting Penny's mother because most of the

people who live there are in wheelchairs and are happy to pet any dog who walks by. I know these visits are harder for Penny, though. Usually she cries on the drive home and sometimes she even cries while we're there.

Once, driving home, she told me, "That woman we just visited wasn't my mother. That isn't the woman I grew up with." At first I was confused and then I understood: She *was* her mother, she'd just *changed* a lot. "She doesn't understand anything. She can barely talk! That's not the mom I remember!"

I never met the mom she remembered, but the woman I met understood a lot more than Penny thought. I could tell by her face and the way she looked me right in the eyes. I knew what she was trying to ask me: *Does she always talk this much? Is it annoying to you, too?*

Now I wonder if she might have been saying those things and I didn't understand back then that some people can hear me and I can hear them. I know I shouldn't get my hopes up. In the last three days, Penny hasn't once mentioned Gus or his family.

Twice, I've heard Sara's voice leaving messages on the answering machine.

At night I've been lying awake on my old bed that still

smells like their house, trying to think of ways to get back home, to Gus and Sara and Marc.

Running away isn't a good option. It takes a few different highways and a long time to drive here. Highways are roads where cars drive faster than anyone can run. Even with my nose, I'm too far away to find them by smell.

I've thought about sneaking out with one of the few visitors who come to Penny's house—the mailman who comes every day maybe, or the garbage collector. But I'm pretty sure if they found me in their truck, they'd bring me back here.

As smart as Penny thinks I am, I can't think of an answer for this.

But visiting her mother has possibilities. It means we'll be in public again. It's a small chance, but maybe I'll see Sara or Marc or Gus. If I do I'll run to them and I won't leave their side. I know this is a very small chance, though.

Maybe I'll see Ms. Winger or Mr. McGregor, who will say, "That dog belongs back at our school."

Maybe they will scare Penny the way people with regular jobs and families seem to.

We hardly talk at all on the drive over. She's nervous about seeing her mother, I can tell. She looks like she's about to start crying just thinking about it, which makes me feel bad.

* * *

The hallways are lined with older people in wheelchairs on their way to their activities. The last time we came, I was an activity, part of a pet-visiting day with two other dogs and a cat who shed white fur onto every lap she sat in. Maybe Penny is remembering this too because as she opens the door she says, "I hope we don't see Snowball today."

Penny's mother looks the same as I remember. She's wearing clothes but lying on top of a made-up bed. Two pink slippers sit on the floor beside her. When we walk in, she opens her eyes. She looks at Penny first and then at me. I'm the one she recognizes first.

"You're back!" she says. She can't remember my name, I can tell, but she remembers me.

"That's right, Mom," Penny says, smiling. "You remember Chester? I've got him back now. He's living with me again. Isn't that great!"

Her mother stares right at me. This is my chance. *I don't belong with Penny,* I say. *I belong to another family. I need to get back to them.*

Her head turns a little. I think she hears me, but she's trying to figure out where the voice is coming from. *Can you tell Penny to take me back to Gus's house?*

233

Her eyes, which have been wandering the room looking for the source of my voice, settle back on me.

It's me talking. Chester. I need your help.

This is hard to manage. Penny is talking at the same time, going on about how "right" it feels to have me home again, how excited her online friends are to meet me and see all the things I can do.

As she talks, her mother looks confused. She shakes her head. "No," she says. "He shouldn't be with you."

Yes! I'm so happy I go over to the bed and lick her hand. *Thank you! I shouldn't be with her.*

Penny says, "No, Mom, it's fine. See, he's wearing his vest. He can come into the building with me. Therapy dogs are allowed in nursing homes."

No. Tell her Gus needs me to go back to school. Tell her I have a job to do.

Her eyes are wandering again. Penny can't stop talking. She tells her mother how special I am, how I can read words, how big my vocabulary is. "I really believe he's going to be famous soon. We'll be watching him on TV, Mom. He's going to be the world's first talking dog."

Not really. I can't talk except to a few people like you. And Gus. That's why he needs me. Without me, he doesn't understand other people very well because he can't talk either. But together we do okay.

It's funny, I think. When someone understands what you're saying, it's such a relief it's hard to stop talking. Penny must feel the same way, because she can't stop talking either.

"I have some people who want to see videos of Chester. My plan is to get him reading about twenty words and then I'll send along a tape of what he can do. I don't want to do it too early while he might still look like a dog doing parlor tricks, you know?"

"What about Gus?" her mother says.

Penny's eyes widen. She hasn't mentioned Gus's name once since we've been here. "What did you say, Mom?"

"He belongs to Gus."

"How do you know that? Has someone been in here talking to you?"

Her mother lifts one of her fingers and points it at me.

Now Penny's really scared. "What are you talking about, Mom?"

"He says Gus needs him to go back to school. I don't know why, though. Do you know what he's talking about?"

How to Speak

PENNY DOESN'T SPEAK THE WHOLE DRIVE home. There are two messages on the answering machine from Sara, asking Penny to please call her as soon as possible. I'm scared this means something has happened to Gus, that maybe he's back in the hospital already.

I don't know what Penny's thinking.

She storms around the kitchen, looking for something. When she knocks over the cardboard tower, she kicks it across the room like she doesn't care anymore about all the time she spent making it.

I don't know if this will help, but I go to the pile of new flash cards we've been working on. I can't read any of them but I remember one of the new ones because it has a picture on it. A mouth with lips.

I pick it up and carry it over to her. She stops being angry for a second and takes it out of my mouth. "Speak?" she says.

She starts to really cry. Not the little tears she cried in the car. These are big sobs. I'm scared she might choke or stop breathing. It looks like maybe she's having a broken heart attack. I don't want Penny to have a broken heart and die. I just want to go back to my family and do my job with Gus.

I move a little closer. She's crumpled up the flash card, so now neither one of us can read it. *It'll be okay*, I tell her. *Take deep breaths.*

I'm surprised.

She takes a deep breath.

That's good, I say.

She takes another.

It's almost like she *can* hear me somewhere, in the back of her mind. Or maybe in her heart she can hear me, she just doesn't listen most of the time because she doesn't like what I have to say. *It will all be okay if you take me back to Gus. I will work hard for him and be the best service dog you ever trained. You'll be proud of me. You'll see.*

She can hear some of this, I'm almost sure. Or at least she can *feel* it.

That's better than being famous.

She takes another deep breath.

I've got to keep going. I can't stop now. *I don't want to be famous like the dog in the video who never gets to eat his bacon.*

I can't believe it. She's stopped crying for long enough to smile for a second. We've watched that video a lot. I've never laughed at it the way Penny does. I always wonder if that poor dog is embarrassed now. How could he not be? Famous for wanting bacon so much that he gets a little whiny. It could happen to any of us. It's funny to some people.

Penny stops smiling. She holds out her hands for me to come over and put my head in her lap. "I'm just going to miss you so much," she says. She's crying again, a little. "I feel like I need you too, but maybe he needs you more."

I lick her face, which always makes her laugh. I don't know if she's heard me or not. All I know is that she's understood enough to know what she needs to do.

How to Go Home

THAT AFTERNOON PENNY STARTS TEACHING me seizure-response protocols. I'm so eager to learn that it doesn't take long. Watching videos helps, except they're all golden retrievers, which scares me a little. The only golden retrievers I've met have always seemed so sure of themselves. Once I saw a golden urinate on another dog's foot. That isn't a sight any dog can easily forget.

After Penny breaks down the tasks I'll need to do when Gus has another seizure, it's not hard to imagine doing this job. When I smell a seizure coming, I need to get him away from staircases and windows. I should have him lie down on the floor so he's less likely to hurt himself falling.

After a seizure, I need to press a button that he'll wear

around his neck to call for help. If he's not wearing the button, or I can't get to it, I need to make sure he's safe and go for help myself.

I haven't done the button part, but I've done all the other things. It surprises me, realizing this, because so far Gus's seizures have always happened when something else stressful is also going on. First the fire alarm, then the fight with Eleanor. Maybe if I remember these times when my instincts were good, I can build up my confidence.

Penny talks a lot about having confidence. It means believing you can do something even if you haven't done it before and you aren't sure. Penny says her problem for most of her life has been not having enough confidence in herself. "I don't want you to have that same problem, too, Chester. Maybe that's why I've worked so hard to show you how smart you are. I want you to believe in yourself the way I do."

Now that we're finally doing the work that will get me back home to Gus, it's easier for me to like Penny again.

You should have confidence, too, I tell her. *Look at the great job you've done with all your dogs! Look at the great job you did with me!*

I don't know if she can hear me the way Gus can and

her mother could. I think my voice sounds like her own thoughts in her head.

"Sometimes I look at the wonderful dogs I've trained—I look at you, Chester, and I think I *should* have more confidence."

It teaches me something. Gus is my person because he can hear me, but I can still help other people I love by sitting near them and thinking positive thoughts. That will never be my main job, but it can be my side job. I think a lot of dogs do this as a side job.

It's an important one too.

Penny is very quiet before she takes me back to Gus. I'm scared that she'll cry, so I don't say anything. I sit as still as possible and try not to think anything either.

I watch Penny take slow trips out to the car with all my things. My bed. My bowls. My sack of food. It's sad, but watching her empty her house of dog things, I get an idea: She should get her own dog! She shouldn't let Wendy or anyone else decide whether she's good enough to have a dog. She should go to one of the places we always see advertised on TV, where thin dogs look out from behind cages with eyes that say, *Will you please bring me home?* Whenever we see one of those commercials, Penny always says, "I can't stand these ads. I can't stand looking at those sweet sad faces on TV."

Once, she said she couldn't adopt one of them because too many sad things had already happened to them. Now, when she walks back into the house after her last trip, I'm sitting by the door waiting for her.

You should adopt your own dog from a shelter, I say, looking into her eyes. *A lot of sad things have happened to me, but you still love me. You should find another dog to keep. You love dogs, and you shouldn't have to always give away the things you love.*

I don't know if she hears me. If she hears, I don't know if she'll follow my suggestion. I think about all the months we lived together. She has a lot of reasons to say no, it wouldn't be a good idea.

She used to talk a lot about neighborhood dogs she didn't like. Poodles are too high-strung, she'd say. Border collies are too hyper, herding anything that moves. Goldens think they're better than everyone else. Penny has many low opinions of other dogs but the lowest of all is for mutts. "You have to watch out for them," she once told me. "You never know what you're getting."

In the car driving to Gus's house, she's very quiet. I take

a risk and say, *You might be wrong about the mutts on TV. Yes, you don't know what you're getting, but that's the exciting part. I didn't know what I was getting when I first met Gus. He was scared of me and I was scared of him, too. Love is when you get to know each other well enough to not be scared anymore.*

I don't know if Penny can hear me.

Her eyes are on the road. She's driving slowly because she doesn't want to get to where we are going.

Eventually we do and Sara opens the door the minute Penny's car pulls into the driveway. "We're so happy to see you again!" she says to me, not Penny. She comes over to my door and opens it because she can't wait anymore.

I bounce around and around like a puppy so she knows I'm happy too.

It's wonderful to be home.

That night, in Gus's room after Sara turns out the light and leaves us alone, Gus talks to me for the first time since I've been back. *Did you go somewhere? It seems like I haven't seen you for a while.*

I think about how frantic I felt and how much I missed him. I wonder if I should be hurt that he hardly noticed I was gone. *No,* I think. *This is my job. He's learning how to* notice people and animals enough to miss them. *I'm teaching him that.*

I tell him, *I wasn't far away. And now I'm back. I won't do that again, I promise. I didn't like being away. I missed you.*

I wait for him to say the same thing to me, but he doesn't.

For a long time he doesn't say anything at all. And then, just as I'm drifting off, he surprises me. *You missed something.*

Oh? What?

One bird flew away. There used to be four. Now there's three.

I sit up a little. I thought he'd forgotten about the bird nest we shared before we started watching TV. When you spend your day looking out the window, the stories are a little slower and less exciting. But they're there. If you look long enough, they're there. Gus taught me that.

Did it die? he asks me now.

Probably, I think to myself. I remember there was a little one who didn't look very strong. *No,* I say. *I think it went back to school to see all its friends.*

Gus sits up in bed, confused.

That was a little joke. Birds don't go to school.

He lies back down. *I don't want to go to school either.*

Think about the parts you liked. Like Mama and her dishwasher. And Amelia.

Who?

Amelia. The girl who comes over to sit with us. She needs a friend, I think. She gets sad and frustrated sometimes. Like you, a little bit.

I do?

Yes. Sometimes.

Okay. I guess I do.

A Real Surprise

THE NEXT MORNING, I WAKE UP to a real surprise: a brand-new orange vest with words written on it. I can't read them, of course, but Sara reads them for me. "Official Service Dog. Please Don't Pet Me. I'm Working Right Now."

Even though it's not the friendliest message in the world, I love the vest more than any present I've ever gotten, including Drubbie, my favorite chew toy, who I accidentally chewed up a long time ago.

I'll never chew this.

At school, I wonder if people will recognize me wearing my new vest, but I'm surprised. Everyone does recognize me! Most of them come over to pet or hug me, then they read my vest and say, "Oh, I'm sorry, Gus—I shouldn't interrupt Chester, should I?"

I like that they talk to Gus about this.

He doesn't answer for now, but maybe someday soon he will. Maybe he'll say, "It's okay," or "Not now." We can work on different possibilities.

For now I won't try to feed him answers or force him to talk the way I did before. People have to decide these things for themselves. The best thing I can do is help when he needs me, and when he doesn't, I can sit near him, thinking positive thoughts.

I'm pretty sure this helps.

Before Penny left our house yesterday, she told Sara that she was thinking about visiting the animal shelter to see if there were any dogs she liked. "That's a wonderful idea!" Sara said. She sounded very happy, like Penny seemed more normal to her now, saying something like this instead of talking too fast about how smart I am and how I can read.

It *is* a more normal thing to say. Dogs can't really read and we can't use flash cards to talk to the people we love, mostly because if we really love them and they love us, we don't need to. We can just sit near each other and listen to our thoughts. Some of them are mine and some of them are his. That's how it works when you find your person.

Unfortunately, when we walk into Ms. Winger's classroom, the first person we see is Ed.

"What's he doing here?" Ed asks when he sees me. "I thought he wasn't allowed anymore."

Seeing him is hard for Gus. This is the first time since something happened in the tunnel that gave Gus two black eyes.

Walk around him, I say.

Gus doesn't hear me. Part of the problem is that Ed is interesting to him. Ed is like the chainsaw guy in the woods. Gus is scared but Gus likes feeling scared sometimes. I get a crazy idea—*maybe Gus can scare him.* Maybe Gus can do something that will frighten Ed enough for him to leave Gus alone after this. *Remember the zombies?* I say. *Remember how you scared them away?*

I know Gus hears me because he holds up his arms in an X and chops the air in front of him. "Nis!" he shouts. Chop, chop, chop. "Nis! Nis!" Chop. Chop. Chop. He looks and sounds weird, which is perfect. Ed takes a step back.

The other kids giggle nervously. Ed backs really far away.

"You're a strange one, Gus," Ed says. He's worried the

other kids are laughing at him, I can tell. Then I realize: They're laughing at him, not at Gus.

With someone who plays strange, scary tricks on other kids, you have to fight back in strange ways. The other kids look at Gus like he's brilliant, chopping the air with his Cross Sticks arms.

Afterward, Amelia comes over to us. "I'm so glad you're back," she says to me, but she's careful to look at Gus while she talks.

Gus doesn't look at her, but he does do something interesting. He takes one of his hands and covers the part on my vest that says, "Please Don't Pet Me. I'm Working."

He's trying to say something. He wants to tell her, It's okay! Come over whenever you want.

That's nice! I say.

And then I stop myself from saying any more.

I don't want to confuse him. He found his own way to talk to her, which means my job is to sit near him and think positive thoughts. You're doing great, I think, but don't say. She's a nice girl, and maybe someday you can invite her to our house and show her our nest.

She'd like that, I think.

We all would.

Author's Note

Dearest Reader,

As any parent of a young child with autism can tell you, nonverbal communication is an essential piece of getting through most days. The idea for *Chester and Gus* came to me after watching our dog, Buddy, and our autistic son, Ethan, have one of these "conversations" when they were alone. Ethan was upset about socks that wouldn't go on easily, and Buddy, trying to help, brought him first a shoe and then—amazingly, considering he wasn't a trained service dog—a different sock. Frustrated, Ethan kept holding up a flat, stop-sign hand at Buddy's offerings as if to say, *Not now, dog. I've got a sock here that doesn't work*. I watched all this, a little heartbroken. I wanted to say: *He's trying to help, Ethan. We all are*. As Ethan got more frustrated and headed toward a meltdown, Buddy hunted through the laundry spread out on the den floor at Ethan's feet and picked up his final offering: a pot holder.

I hooted from the corner and even Ethan had to laugh. A crisis was averted without a word.

Buddy was not a service school dropout dog when he joined our family, but as I did research for this book and watched the extraordinary work service dogs do—fueled by an innate desire to serve "their person," they almost always do more than they were originally trained for—I realized Buddy shared one essential trait with these dogs: He cared more about helping, comforting, and cheering his family than he did about himself. Even toward the end of his life, after he got cancer, it was clear: He worried more about us and our sadness than about his own pain.

I wrote this story from Chester's point of view because watching Ethan through Buddy's eyes gave me a new, much-needed perspective at a crucial time in our lives when I feared Ethan would never make any real bonds. I gave Chester and Gus their own mysterious connection because I believe animals can provide this, especially for children who most need it. Watching Buddy and Ethan over the years taught me (a writer, who has overvalued language, I'm sure) about how we express love when words aren't available, or even an option. I wanted *Chester and Gus* to be a celebration of what I've learned as a parent: bonds formed without words are as meaningful and durable as those created on a river of chatter. Dogs have taught us all that eyes speak volumes and love can be conveyed in perfect silence. What an essential lesson that is for parents of children who communicate in their own mysterious ways.

Best,

Cammie McGovern

Don't miss this heartwarming novel
from Cammie McGovern!

ONE

MY MOM HAS A THEORY THAT when bad things happen, you should think about someone else's problems and try to help them. Like even if you're losing a soccer game terribly you should try to help the poor guy wearing glasses on the other team who just fell down. Things like that. One problem with Mom's theory is that my older brother George is autistic, which means he can't really think about anyone else, much less help them. The other problem is that ever since this summer and what happened to Dad, I don't think anyone else has more problems than we do.

What happened to Dad this summer wasn't my fault.

The first night that Mom came home from the hospital,

she said this to me, and she's been saying it ever since, which of course makes me feel like it *was* my fault, at least a little bit.

The morning that it happened, Dad asked me if I wanted to go to the high school to work on my bike riding. Which was embarrassing because *I'm in fourth grade now.* Of course I can *ride a bike.* Sort of. I just have a hard time starting. And stopping. It also makes me a little nervous slowing down to make turns.

I wasn't always this way. I could ride a bike when I was in second grade like everyone else. Maybe I kept my training wheels on longer than other kids but eventually I let my dad take them off and I made it up and down the street a bunch of times, Dad jogging next to me, Mom taking pictures. I would have said I was a fine bike rider until the end of that summer when we had a bike parade at our block party. We have twelve kids on our block, most of them younger than us, so every bike was decorated with streamers and pom-poms. Stephanie up the street is a year younger than I am, but she had taped pinwheels to her handlebars, which was such a good idea I was jealous. Especially when I saw how they spun like crazy when she rode fast. All I had for deco-ration was a few streamers flapping and two balloons tied to my handlebars, but they weren't doing much. Anyone could see Stephanie's pinwheels were going to win, which made me so mad, I pedaled really hard and fast, *bam!* right into a parked car. I flew into the street and the whole bike parade stopped so everyone could get off their bikes and gather around in a circle to see if I was still alive.

I was. Barely.

Afterward Martin, my oldest brother who's in ninth grade now, kept saying it didn't look that bad. "It was a little funny, actually," he said. "Kind of like a sight gag."

He was trying to make me feel better because it wasn't funny at all.

For a long time afterward, I didn't get on my bike. Even when Martin and his friends built a bike jump out of wood planks and cement blocks, I pretended my foot was hurt so I wouldn't have to do it. When they did races up the street, I would say I heard my mom calling me, so no one would ask why I wasn't racing.

The week before school started this year, Dad called me outside to say he had an idea. "I'm going for a run over at the high school. No one will be there. The track there is a great place to practice riding your bike. No curbs to worry about. No cars to run into . . ."

He clapped his hands like coaches do at halftime when their team is losing.

"I don't know, Dad," I said.

I felt bad for him. When he was a boy, Dad went to a prep school where everyone had to wear ties to class and play a sport every season, even if they were terrible at it. "I hated it. I wouldn't wish that on any of you," he always tells us, but sometimes I wonder if he wishes his sons were a little more like the jocks he says he never liked.

Dad has been an assistant coach on all of our soccer teams, which means his hardest job every year has been thinking up new words to describe our performance when he hands out end-of-the-season trophies. "Benny has worked so hard with the skills he has," he'll say. Or "Benny has been trying to reach a new level of playing. This year he almost has." He says these things because at trophy ceremonies you're not allowed to say the truth, which is "Benny hasn't touched a ball in a game once all season." He also can't say, "Benny seems remarkably uninterested in this sport in spite of all the years I've put in as an assistant coach."

I think if Dad had his secret dream come true, he'd have one of us be a surprisingly good athlete so he could stand on the sidelines of games and say, "It didn't come from me! I'm a terrible athlete!"

Instead he has my brother Martin, who plays basketball because this year he's the tallest boy in ninth grade, but even Martin will admit he's a terrible shooter and anyone in their right mind doesn't throw the ball to him. He also has George, who plays in Special Olympics basketball, where it's okay to just carry the ball from one end of the court to the other without dribbling at all. And me, Benny, who can only ride a bike if someone is there to help me start and stop.

"I don't think that sounds like such a good idea, Dad," I told him after he suggested bike riding at the high school track. I don't know if he realized this, but I hadn't ridden my bike once since the bike parade. I'd *walked* my bike places, and when I got there, I *pretended* I'd rode, but I hadn't actually gotten on my bike and pedaled it since my crash.

"It'll be fun," Dad said. "I'll be right there. Running my laps."

The way he said this, I could tell that he *did* know that I hadn't been on my bike in two years. Mom came outside and they looked at each other like they'd talked about it ahead of time. Like they were both really worried about this, which made me feel *terrible*.

"Okay," I said. "I guess I could try."

Mom hugged me right away. "That's wonderful, Benny! We're so proud of you!"

That afternoon, we got out to the track early while it was still deserted, which was lucky because it turned out that I was even worse than I remembered. Walking over, Dad told me there was an old saying about how you have to get right back on your bike when you fall off. "Or maybe that's a horse," he said. "But the point is you shouldn't wait a year to get back onto whatever you fell off of."

That was a nice idea, except the first time I tried pedaling, I veered right off the track and onto the grass. I don't know if this is true for other people, but whenever I fall off my bike, I'm always sure, for about thirty seconds, that I've broken my leg. There are so many bars that could crush a leg that I can never believe it hasn't happened.

I lay there for a while, looking up at sky, waiting to experience what a broken leg feels like. *It's okay,* I told myself. *If it's broken, I won't have to ride this stupid bike again for a long, long time.*

Then came the bad news.

"Looks like you're okay!" Dad said. "Good to go! Right back in the saddle!" He leaned over. His face was a little red from the effort of staying upbeat. "You're okay, right?"

6

"I think so."

"Super! Why don't I hold the seat while you start pedaling?"

It's embarrassing to be nine years old and have your dad hold your bike seat while you climb on. It's also embarrassing to have him run beside you screaming, "You're veering! You're veering! Make your adjustment!"

But here was the surprise: once I got going, I was fine!

Better than fine! I flew around the track, lightning fast.

I made it around one whole lap while Dad watched me, clapping and cheering. He was right—the track was a great place to practice. I didn't have to worry about running into anything except painted lines on the ground. I got my speed up and practiced staying in between two lines, which was hard, so I gave myself two lanes, which wasn't hard at all.

I couldn't believe how good I was, especially compared to Dad, after he started jogging. Dad didn't really run laps. He shuffled at this strange pace where his legs looked like they were running but old women walked faster. "It's not about speed," he always said, which in his case was certainly true. He looked like he was running backward compared to me.

Poor Dad had to sweat and huff and shuffle to get around the track three times and I lost count after ten. I felt great, like maybe I should become a professional bike rider. Then I saw a woman up ahead on the track, running with her dog. The dog was on a leash, but he liked the inside lane and she liked the outside lane so there was a line stretched like a fence across the track. If I ran into that line, I was sure it would chop me in half, which made me panic and forget how to stop.

I stuck both legs out and yanked the hand brakes, which meant I didn't slow down gradually. My bike stopped but my body didn't. I flew headfirst over the handlebars. I saw the ground, then the sky, then nothing at all.

At the last minute I guess my dad came up behind to help me. His head hit my helmet. Or maybe my head hit his shoulder and he fell back and hit the track. We never figured out exactly what happened. When we got up, a little dazed, he seemed fine. He was more worried about me.

He walked my bike back to the car and drove us home, where he had me lie down on the sofa while he looked up the signs of a concussion, because even though there are three boys in our family, none of us is athletic enough to have ever gotten one.

"Do you feel like throwing up?" he called from his office, where the computer is.

"I don't think so."

"Do you feel dizzy or confused or lethargic?"

"What's lethargic?"

"Tired."

"Sort of."

"Do you have double vision or a vague feeling of mal-aise?"

"What's that?"

"Feeling gloomy."

"A little," I say.

Then—this part is hard for me to think about—while he was still asking my symptoms and reading about concussions on the screen, he slid out of his chair and hit the floor with a thud. I will never forget that sound even if I try to for the rest of my life. Mom heard it, too, and ran into the room. When she couldn't wake him up, she called out for Martin to please call 911.

Don't miss these books by
Cammie McGovern!

Everyone has bad days.
You have to make the good ones.

JUST my LUCK

Cammie McGovern

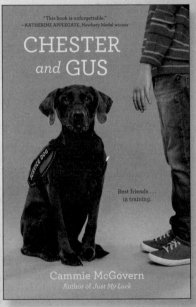

"This book is unforgettable."
—KATHERINE APPLEGATE, Newbery Medal winner

CHESTER
and GUS

Best friends...
in training.

Cammie McGovern
Author of *Just My Luck*

HARPER
An Imprint of HarperCollinsPublishers

www.harpercollinschildrens.com